ALSO BY MATTHEW J. KIRBY

THE QUANTUM LEAGUE

BOOK ONE: SPELL ROBBERS

BY

MATTHEW J. KIRBY

SCHOLASTIC PRESS
New York

Library of Congress Cataloging-in-Publication Data
Kirby, Matthew J., 1976–
Spell robbers / by Matthew J. Kirby. — First edition.
pages cm. — (The Quantum League ; Book one)
Summary: Ben Warner is invited to join a "science camp" led by a
quantum physicist Dr. Madeleine Hughes, and with his new friend
Peter he discovers the secret art of actuation — the ability to change
reality by imagining it differently — but he also finds that there are
people willing to kill for that secret.
ISBN 978-0-545-50226-9 (jacketed hardcover) 1. Imagination — Juvenile
fiction. 2. Quantum theory — Juvenile fiction. 3. Physicists —
Juvenile fiction. 4. Friendship — Juvenile fiction. 5. Adventure stories.
[1. Science fiction. 2. Imagination — Fiction. 3. Quantum theory —
Fiction. 4. Physicists — Fiction. 5. Friendship — Fiction. 6. Adventure
and adventurers — Fiction.] I. Title.
PZ7.K633528Spe 2014
813.6 — dc23
2013013216

10 9 8 7 6 5 4 3 2 1   14 15 16 17 18

Printed in the U.S.A.   23
First edition, February 2014
The text type was set in Apollo MT.
The display type was set in Bonn.
Book design by Phil Falco and Abby Kuperstock
Author photo by Naomi Leu

For Jeanne Kirby,
who taught me to believe in magic.

CHAPTER
1

THE empty cafeteria table snapped in half at the middle and shot up off the ground. Its hinges shrieked as the whole table slammed shut, spinning a little on its wheels. All on its own.

Ben leaped away from it, stunned, while the rest of the students in the cafeteria fell silent. Everyone stared at the table like it might open back up and attack any one of them, including the guy who'd just been threatening to beat Ben into the ground. Ben had only been at this school for two weeks, and he'd already run afoul of the class bully. But the table seemed to have changed that, at least for the moment.

Ben felt a tug on his arm as a boy came up and pulled him away.

"Move." The kid nodded toward the cafeteria's double doors.

Ben followed him, but glanced back a couple of times at the table. The bully was still staring at it.

Out in the common area, Ben asked the kid, "Did you see that?"

"Yeah, I saw." He shrugged, wearing a T-shirt printed with WANTED: SCHRODINGER'S CAT, DEAD AND ALIVE. "Perfect timing, wouldn't you say?"

"I . . . guess so. But what if somebody had been sitting on that thing?"

"I'm Peter."

"I — I'm Ben."

"I know. You're in my third period." Peter turned and walked away, threading the crowded common area with ease, without touching or interacting with anyone.

Ben got lost on his way home.

He couldn't find his own apartment. True, they'd only moved to town a couple of weeks ago, but still. He should've known better. After all the places they'd lived, he *did* know better, yet there he was, wandering the sprawling and utterly confusing campus family-housing grounds, trying to look like he knew where he was going. The apartments were clustered in two-story buildings, arranged haphazardly, a maze of sidewalks running among them.

At one point, Ben actually thought he'd found it, but realized quickly it was the wrong place when his key didn't work. Then he heard a stirring on the other side of the door, probably because whoever it was had heard him jiggling the lock, and he hurried away.

He eventually spotted a sad little playground he recognized. The sand was mixed with things that weren't sand, and packed down hard. He remembered seeing the edge of it from his bedroom window, so he figured out the right angle and headed in that direction.

When he finally got home, Ben felt and heard the scrape of cardboard boxes on the other side of the front door as he tried to push it open. His mom was still unpacking. The apartment was paid for by her scholarship. It was small, but it was newer and cleaner than some of the other places they'd lived.

"Mom?" Ben squeezed through the opening.

"In my room!"

Ben tossed his backpack onto the couch that was still missing a cushion, and went past the little kitchen to his mom's bedroom. She stood by the bed, where she had laid out a bunch of clothes Ben recognized from the last time she'd gone to school. Back then it was a master's degree in art history. This time, if she finished, it was going to be a master's degree in medieval literature. She would never use either.

She scanned the bed, her hands on her hips. "I hope

these still fit. I can't exactly wear my stained overalls as a teaching assistant." She looked up. "How was your day? Still liking your school?"

"Sure."

Between the last graduate program and this one, they'd lived in an art commune where Ben's mom worked on a blueberry farm and did found-object sculpting on the side, and the overalls she wore every day showed it.

She picked up a navy blouse and held it out in front of her by the shoulders. "Make any friends?"

"Maybe. This kid Peter kind of helped me out."

"With what?"

"Just some guy."

She brought the shirt down to her waist. "This other guy hassling you?"

"Not bad."

She looked him in the eyes. He looked back. She did this thing where if she wanted to know more, she'd just sit and stare, trying to wait it out of him. Ben had learned he could outlast her. And the last thing she needed to worry about the night before starting classes was some bully at school. He smiled.

She gave up and turned her attention back to the bed. "You let me know if it becomes a problem."

"I will."

She shook out a pair of black pants. "Are you hungry? What do you want for dinner?"

Ben turned for the door. She didn't need to worry about that right now, either. "I'll go see what we have. You keep getting ready."

"Thanks."

In the kitchen, he opened up the cupboard and dug around until he found a jar of spaghetti sauce. Then he found some noodles. It took a few minutes to locate a pan in one of the unpacked boxes, but he filled it up with water and got it on the stove.

By the time the noodles were done and dished up on plates, his mom came out of her bedroom in a T-shirt, pulling the strings tight on her sweats. "Oh, good. Thanks for making dinner." Ben lifted the hot jar of sauce from the microwave with a couple of pot holders and poured it over the noodles. "Don't worry about making your lunch," she said. "I'll take care of that later!"

Ben smiled and grabbed the can of Parmesan cheese from the fridge. "All right, Mom."

They sat down at their table. And it *was* their table. His mom had salvaged it from a local burger place that went out of business. This was two cities ago, and they'd eaten there a lot — great hand-cut fries — until the owners had decided to retire and sell everything. Including the table Ben and his mom had always shared. "So tell me about Peter," his mom said.

Ben twisted some noodles onto his fork. "He seems kinda weird."

"Weird how?"

"He's a loner."

She smiled at the corner of her mouth. "Well, I just hope you make at least one good friend. We'll be here for a while. The program is at least two years."

He wanted to believe her. "I hope your classes go okay tomorrow."

They both ate a few bites.

"Anything else happen today?" she asked.

Ben looked at his fork. "Something weird happened in the cafeteria."

"Oh?"

"Yeah. One of those heavy tables just lifted up out of nowhere and snapped shut."

His mom put down her fork. "Was anyone hurt?"

"No." *But almost.*

"Well, that's good. It sounds like it could have been worse."

"Yeah." It could have been much worse, but the table was empty. *Perfect timing.*

"Oh," his mom said. "I found something you might be interested in."

"What's that?"

"A professor on campus e-mailed asking if you'd like to attend her science camp after school."

"Science camp?" That could go either way, but Ben was betting on it being a waste of time. "Why'd she e-mail about me?"

"She said someone at your school had recommended you. It sounded pretty advanced. Something about quantum mechanics. I don't think you'll be bored."

"No, thanks."

She leaned forward, her hands folded around her plate. "Would you at least go check it out? It would make me feel better knowing you had someplace to go after school. And it's on campus, not too far from all my classes."

"Is it expensive?" Ben knew they couldn't afford any extras right now.

"It's free."

Ben sighed. "Okay. If it will make you feel better."

"Thank you. They hold it in that building everyone calls the Castle. You can start tomorrow. Oh, and there's some kind of test to get in."

"A test?"

"Yeah, but I'm sure you'll do fine."

Ben already regretted agreeing to it, but at this point the best way to handle his mom would be to go at least once. It would be easier to come up with a reason to quit than a reason not to try it.

They finished dinner, and as Ben carried the dishes to the sink, he noticed a pale green pill sitting on the counter by the sink.

"Mom."

"What?"

He pinched the pill in his fingertips and brought it to her. "You forgot again."

"Oh, right." She took it from him and swallowed it down without any water. "I set it down this morning when I spilled some coffee. Guess I forgot."

So long as she didn't forget too many days in a row, it wasn't a big deal.

Ben had been on plenty of college campuses before, sitting in libraries and study rooms, when he was younger and his mom couldn't find or afford a babysitter. So he felt pretty comfortable walking across the Quad to the Castle after school.

He was headed for an old three-story brick structure with granite window casements, towers, and a high peaked roof. The building's nickname was appropriate, but not terribly original. It had to be the oldest building at the university.

Inside the Castle, dark, rich wood paneled the walls hung with old black-and-white historical photos of buildings that looked forever haunted, and men and women who never seemed to smile and had shadows for eyes. The Castle's floors looked like they had once been tiled with marble or stone, but were so scuffed and dingy, it might as well have been linoleum.

The directions told him to go to the basement level, which Ben guessed could be called the Dungeon. He found a staircase and went down to the basement level, where there were no windows — just the kind of fluorescent lighting that buzzed and gave Ben's mom headaches.

He followed a long hallway, his footsteps echoing, and ahead of him Ben saw an open doorway. Light and voices spilled out through it, and he figured that was where he was supposed to go.

Ben rounded the door and went into a larger room than he had been expecting. It looked like the university had knocked down a few walls and combined several class-rooms into one. Around the space, strips of colored tape on the floor marked off different stations and areas. Tripods mounted with what looked like little satellite dishes stood in circles around the areas, and wires snaked across the floor, creating a web between the dozen or so computers scattered around the room.

This already looked different from any of the after-school programs he'd attended.

Off to one side, a woman stood in front of a semicircle of six folding metal chairs. She was small, with short gray hair, smooth skin, and big round eyes. Ben's mom would have called her "elfin." Two of the folding chairs were empty. In the others sat two girls and two boys, all about Ben's age. They turned to look at him, and Ben was surprised to see Peter, the kid from school, among them.

The woman had been talking as Ben walked in, but turned her attention to him now as he stood in the doorway. "Are you Ben?"

"Yup."

"Wait in the hallway, please," she said. "I'll be right with you."

Ben frowned. "Okay."

As he stood outside the room, unable to hear what was going on inside, he thought about just taking off. Before he made up his mind, the woman joined him.

"Thank you for your patience, Ben." She carried a sensor wand that looked a bit like the chirping, squealing metal detectors they used in airports. "I'm so sorry for the wait. I am Dr. Hughes. Welcome."

"Thanks."

"I was the one who contacted your mother, based on Peter's recommendation. You know him from school, I believe?"

So that was what had happened. Maybe it wasn't an accident that Peter had helped him out. "Yeah, I know him."

"Wonderful. Now, before I admit you to the program, I just have to run a simple test."

"What kind of test?"

"An aptitude test."

"Aptitude? Like an IQ test?"

"I suppose so. But I am a quantum physicist, not a psychologist." Dr. Hughes raised the sensor wand. "This will be a simple visualization exercise in which you will picture something I describe for you. I want you to use your imagination to make it as detailed as you can. Your eyes will be closed, but I will be using this device to measure the environment around us. This device is not measuring you or affecting you in any way."

This was weird. "Okay . . ."

"Close your eyes."

Ben hesitated. "What does this have to do with science camp?"

"All will be explained. Please close your eyes."

Ben did.

"I want you to picture the hallway in front of you," Dr. Hughes said. "Just as it was before you closed your eyes. Can you see it?"

"Yes."

"Now, I want you to picture a small spark in the air. As if someone has just struck a match. And the spark is beginning to grow. It's consuming the oxygen in the air, getting larger, hotter. Now, it's a ball of fire."

Ben tried to imagine what she described. It was hard at first, because he kept thinking about her wand thing waving around him. But he worked to put it out of his mind and concentrate. He imagined the fireball hissing and crackling, sucking up the air around it. He could see the colors, blue at the center, then yellow, then red at the edges of the flames. He imagined the heat it was throwing off, and could almost feel it against his face. He started to think that if he opened his eyes, the fireball would be right there in front of him, churning and scorching the air.

"Open your eyes, Ben."

He did.

No fireball.

Dr. Hughes lowered the sensor wand. "Excellent!"

"Did I pass?"

"Indeed, you did. Very strong indications of aptitude. The highest I have seen to date."

That sounds good, whatever it means. "So, what happens now?"

"Now we begin. You may join the others."

Ben nodded and reentered the classroom, but stopped short a foot into the room, stunned by what he saw. Peter stood in the middle of a circle of tripods, holding out his hands. Between his hands burned a small fireball the size of a grapefruit.

Not an imaginary fireball.

A *real* fireball.

CHAPTER
2

BEN didn't know what to think or say. He just stood there with his mouth open, watching the fireball burn in front of Peter for another moment before it vanished with a puff of smoke. The other three kids stood outside the tripods, acting like nothing unusual was going on.

"Excellent, Peter," Dr. Hughes said. "But we were supposed to work on water today."

Peter nodded. "Right. Sorry, Dr. Hughes."

"That's quite all right. Class, I'd like you to meet our newest member, Ben."

They all turned to face him.

"Ben, this is Julie, Abbie, and Dylan. Peter you know, of course."

"Hey," Ben said to them, and they said "hey" back.

"We're just getting started for the day." Dr. Hughes gestured Ben toward the metal folding chairs. "While I conduct a brief orientation with Ben, I'd like for the rest of you to begin. Focus on condensation. Clouds and rain. Do you think you could lead the exercises, Peter?"

"Absolutely, Dr. Hughes."

"Excellent." Dr. Hughes led Ben away from the circle.

He didn't want to go. He wanted to stay and watch Peter. Ben didn't quite believe what he'd seen. But Dr. Hughes guided him with a hand against his back, and then pointed at one of the chairs. "Please, have a seat."

Ben lowered himself slowly onto the cold metal chair, watching Peter.

Dr. Hughes took a chair next to him. "I can see you're distracted. Before we begin, let's watch for a moment."

Peter strode to the middle of the tripods and closed his eyes. He held his hands in front of him, wide, like he was holding a huge beach ball. And he just stood there.

"What's he doing?" Ben asked.

"Just watch," Dr. Hughes said.

A few moments passed, and then something happened. Between Peter's hands, a little smudge appeared. Within seconds it had swelled to a wisp, and moments later, a puff. Then it was a cloud. A little cloud. Ben blinked. It was still there.

He stood up. "Okay, what's going on?"

"Physics," Dr. Hughes said.

Ben looked at her. "Physics?"

"Physics."

The little cloud had grown even larger between Peter's hands, and it had darkened in the center, getting denser. And then, a drop of water fell from it and splashed on the floor. Then another, and another.

Rain.

It was raining. Before long, Peter stood in a small puddle, his pants wet in spots below his knees. A moment later, he opened his eyes and flung his arms wide, as if letting the little storm cloud go free. It dissipated quickly, leaving only the wet floor behind.

Peter looked across the room at Ben. He smiled. Ben smiled back. He had no idea what he had just seen. But it was amazing. And if *this* was what they did here at this science camp, then Ben was thrilled he'd gotten in. But how was it possible?

He turned back to Dr. Hughes. "I don't understand. How did —?"

"You're very bright, Ben." Dr. Hughes reached over and tapped the chair where Ben had been sitting. "What do you know about quantum mechanics?"

But he couldn't sit. Not right now. And he didn't want a science lesson, either. "Not much. It's physics for really small stuff, right? Electrons and quarks and stuff like that."

"Yes, that is the conventional understanding. Basically, the laws that govern larger objects, like planets and basketballs, start to break down when we get to the smallest of scales. That's when things get very, very strange."

Ben knew this was a science camp and all, but a lecture? Really? Now? After what he'd just seen Peter do?

"Look, Dr. Hughes, I —"

She silenced him with an upheld finger. She really was a teacher. "Quantum mechanics inform our understanding and predictions for many things. Every natural process, whether chemical, or biological, or astronomical, ultimately comes back to quantum physics. As strange as it is, the math works perfectly, and because of that, we have things like lasers and microprocessors."

Ben felt a growl of frustration rumbling just under his breath. "Okay."

"Have you heard of quantum entanglement?"

"No."

"It is possible for two particles to become what we call entangled, such that their states are inextricably linked. The measurement of one particle *instantly* affects the state of the other particle, whether they are in the same room, or even on different *planets*. The particles are connected. Are you with me?"

Ben didn't see how that could be. He thought nothing moved faster than the speed of light. "So when you say 'instantly' . . ."

"I mean instantly. No matter the distance."

This was new to Ben. "But what does this have to do with that?" He pointed in Peter's direction.

"Well, in some ways, everything in this world is connected through entanglement. Any two objects that have interacted become entangled on a level we can't perceive and find difficult to measure. All the universe is a great bubbly fabric, and you are a part of the pattern, down to your atoms."

This was starting to sound kind of hokey. Ben probably would have walked out at that point if he hadn't just seen what he had seen.

"'Thou canst not stir a flower without troubling of a star,'" Dr. Hughes said.

"What?"

"It's a poem."

Even more hokey.

Dr. Hughes continued. "It means that small disturbances can have tremendous, even unimaginable consequences. There are certain people, Ben, whom we call Actuators. They have the ability to disturb the universal fabric with their thoughts, to *actuate* an event. So long as we have the proper equipment."

Ben looked back at Peter. "So Peter is a — an Actuator?"

"Yes. Someone who can focus his or her thoughts in such a way that the entanglement of his or her consciousness with the world brings about events. Like that rain cloud."

"Like being psychic?"

Dr. Hughes pursed her lips. "I prefer you not use that term. And I don't like the term 'magic,' either. They are not scientifically accurate."

"Okay. But that's basically what it is, right?"

"I suppose."

"So what are those doing?" Ben pointed at the tripods.

"Those are augmenting devices. They reflect and magnify the quantum energy radiating from Peter. That is how he was able to do what you saw. Without them, he would not be able to actuate that cloud."

"Can you actuate things without them?"

"No. My equipment is what makes actuation possible."

This was unbelievable, and Ben was confused. "How can the rest of the world not know about this?"

"When the idea of actuation was theoretical," Dr. Hughes said, "I was laughed at by my colleagues. We've now gone beyond theory, but the technology isn't perfected. Before I go public, I have to make sure the data and evidence are unassailable. But I do hope to make an announcement in the next six months. Until then, I expect you to keep this a secret." Dr. Hughes looked at him from under her brow. "Understood?"

"Understood," Ben said.

"Excellent. Then let's begin your first lesson."

A few minutes later, Ben stood inside one of the tripod rings. Dr. Hughes and Ben's classmates stood outside the circle.

It felt to Ben like he was on some kind of stage, with bright lights and an audience staring at him, and he did not want to trip.

"The key to actuation," Dr. Hughes said, "is how fully you realize the event you are trying to bring about. Like the visualization exercise I just had you do in the hallway."

Ben took a deep breath. "Okay."

"The more detailed your visualization, the more complete your thought, the greater the chances of actuation. That means understanding all the consequences, all the precursors, everything about the event that you can."

"Got it."

"So now." Dr. Hughes went to stand in front of one of the computer monitors. "I'd like you to close your eyes."

Ben did.

"Relax," she said. "Take a few deep breaths. Hold your hands out in front of you, like you saw Peter do. And now picture a cloud between them. Imagine the moisture condensing out of the air, molecules collecting."

Ben saw what she described. He turned his normal vision into science-documentary animation, zooming in on the atoms floating in the air around him, the hydrogen and the oxygen. He grabbed two hydrogen, one oxygen, and stuck them together, and he imagined others coming together, too. Hundreds, thousands, millions more. Together, they became a mist, and then a cloud, and then falling water droplets, all between his hands.

Suddenly, he became aware that the room was silent around him. He became aware of his feet squishing inside his tennis shoes, and the coldness of wet jeans against his shins. He opened his eyes.

A charcoal cloud the size of a car churned in the air in front of him. It stretched to the edges of the circle, flooding the floor with rain even as Ben's excitement burned hot. This was power. This was control. In *his* hands.

The others had all stepped away from it. They looked back and forth between the cloud and Ben with fear in their eyes. Except Peter. Peter was looking past the cloud, right at Ben, his expression blank.

Dr. Hughes's fingers flicked over her keyboard. "Good. That's good, Ben. And now I need you to disperse the water in your cloud back into the air, just as you collected it."

The cloud flashed with an angry little bolt of lightning.

"Close your eyes," Dr. Hughes said. "Before it gets away from you."

"Gets away from me?" Ben asked.

"Just do as I say." Dr. Hughes's voice sounded calm, but strained. Was she afraid, too?

Ben closed his eyes. He pictured the cloud in his mind, and focused on its molecules. He cracked the bonds holding them together and broke them into atoms, just as he'd assembled them, and scattered them like smoke until they'd dissipated.

He opened his eyes. The cloud was gone. But the floor was still wet. "How was that?" he asked.

No one said anything. They just stared. Like they were still afraid. But not Peter.

Dr. Hughes cleared her throat. "Class, you will continue practicing your exercises. Ben and I will return shortly."

Return? Where were they going?

"Yes, Dr. Hughes." Peter smiled at her, and then cast a dark look at Ben. Was he angry about something?

"Come, Ben." Dr. Hughes waved for him to follow and led him through the classroom door into the hallway. "Let's go up to my office, shall we?"

"All right."

They climbed the stairs to the first floor, and then up to the second, past more creepy old photographs. The wooden steps creaked a little under their feet on their way up to the third. The ceiling on that floor slanted, giving Ben the feeling of needing to duck his head. They walked down a narrow hallway to its end, where Dr. Hughes unlocked a door.

The room inside was round, and lined with shelves and shelves of books. A desk overflowing with papers stood before a single slit of a window, straight ahead.

"Are we in a tower?" he asked.

Dr. Hughes glanced around. "Yes. I asked for this office. I don't like corners. Things get stuck in corners. Please, sit down." She motioned toward one of two chairs in front of her desk, and she took her place on the opposite side.

Ben sat. "Am I in trouble?"

"No, no, Ben. Nothing like that."

"Then why —?"

"I'm sure you took note of how the others reacted to your actuation."

"Yeah, I guess so."

"The fact is, none of them, not even Peter, has actuated anything remotely close to that. And they have been practicing for weeks and months. You were able to do that on your first try. It's quite astonishing."

Ben kept his pride from turning into a smile. But then, what she'd said made him wonder something. "Can you actuate, Dr. Hughes?"

She smiled down at her desk. "No, Ben. I can't. I haven't found an adult who can."

"Why not?"

"I think it has to do with imagination. Adult brains have already decided long ago what's possible and what's not." Her eyes watered up, and her voice got quiet. "But actuation would have meant a great deal to me when I was your age."

Ben looked away, unsure of what she meant or what he should say.

Dr. Hughes cleared her throat. "During the actuation, I told you it could get away from you. Do you remember?"

"Yes." Ben leaned forward, grateful for a change of subject. "What did you mean by that?"

"In the beginning, it was your thoughts that created and sustained that cloud. But if you had let it go long enough, or get big enough, eventually, there would have come a tipping point when the cloud would have ceased being an actuation and become an actual cloud."

"What's the difference?" Ben's cloud seemed plenty actual to him.

"An actuation is still just the physical manifestation of a potential, one remote possibility. But an actual thing isn't potential anymore. It's there, and it has a material life of its own. A runaway train."

"So what happens if it gets away from me?"

Dr. Hughes shook her head. "Who knows? Bigger cloud. More rain. Lightning. It hasn't been a high enough risk to worry about until today."

"I see." But inside, Ben wasn't worried. The cloud had felt completely under his control. It hadn't felt like a runaway train at all.

"I'm glad you understand," Dr. Hughes said. "Knowing what I know now about your gift, I'll be better prepared next time. We'll take it slowly. Cautiously. You're very unique, Ben. Who knows what you might accomplish."

CHAPTER
3

AFTER class, Ben walked with Peter to the bus stop. Ben didn't plan to ride the bus, but it was on the way to where he was meeting his mom. It was a busy time of day, and they moved with a tide of college students.

"What did you think?" Peter asked.

"I don't know what to think," Ben said.

Peter nodded. "That'll pass."

Ben didn't see that happening. How could you get used to this? "Why'd you give Dr. Hughes my name in the first place?"

"When we met at school, I could tell you were an Actuator."

"How?"

"You start to sense it after you've practiced for a while."

"Well," Ben said. "Thanks."

"You're welcome. Since I got you in, maybe you could do something for me."

"What?"

"Tell me how you did that with the cloud. I've never seen an actuation that big before."

Ben shrugged. "I don't know."

"Yeah, right. Your first time? That was too good."

"Really. I'd tell you if I knew."

Peter frowned. "Okay."

They arrived at the stop, but the bus hadn't come yet. Peter took a seat under a Plexiglas awning papered with homemade flyers for local bands.

Ben stood in front of him. "So I guess I'll see you at school tomorrow?"

"I eat lunch in the library."

Library? "Um . . ." Ben might not have made any friends yet, might not ever make any real friends while he was at that school, but that didn't mean he wanted to throw in with the outcasts. But as soon as the thought occurred, he felt guilty. Peter was the reason Ben was here. *Actuating.* The least Ben could do was hang out with him for one lunch. "Okay," he said. "I'll come find you."

The bus pulled up then, with its squealing brakes and rock-tumbler engine, and Peter took a step toward it. The door hissed open, and then he climbed up the steps and took a seat. Ben watched it pull away through the black cloud of its own exhaust.

His mom's words echoed in his ear. *At least one good friend.*

But thoughts of lunch reminded him of the cafeteria table, and Ben suddenly wondered if Peter — and actuation — had been involved in that.

Ben's mom brought home pizza that night, the kind you have to bake yourself. She slid it into the oven and collapsed onto the sofa, where she slumped with one elbow up on the sofa's arm, her hand resting over her eyes.

"Could you set the timer, Ben?"

"How long?"

"I don't know. Fifteen minutes?"

He double-checked the directions on the packaging and set the timer for twenty.

"How was the science camp?" she asked.

"It was . . . fun." Ben wasn't sure how much he should share with her. He was still trying to understand what had happened. The whole thing was back to seeming unbelievable to him now, just a few hours later. Like he had imagined it.

Did the other kids' parents know? How could they not? How could you keep it a secret? But standing there, Ben imagined how that conversation would go.

Hey, Mom, guess what? At science camp today I created a rain cloud out of thin air!

Right, Ben. A rain cloud.

No, really! I created a rain cloud!

Fine. I get it. You don't have to tell me about science camp if you don't want to.

And he imagined it would sound something like that for every kid and parent. He wouldn't have believed it if Peter had told him about it before Ben actually saw it. But even if Ben's mom did believe him, wouldn't that just get her all worried about safety and stuff? He figured it was probably best to just stay quiet.

"Fun how?" his mom asked.

"What? Oh, just interesting. I think it'll be good."

"Make any friends there?"

"Maybe," Ben said. "That guy Peter was there. But . . . he eats lunch in the library."

"What's wrong with that?" His mom smiled. "I'm grateful it will give you something to do in the afternoons." She sighed. That deep sigh usually meant trouble and it made Ben nervous.

He almost didn't want to ask, but he did. "How was class?"

"Oh . . . the world is too small."

Ben tensed up. *Not yet.* It couldn't be happening this soon. They'd practically just gotten here, and now Ben had discovered actuation. She couldn't quit yet. They couldn't move again.

"What —?" Ben shook his head. "What do you mean?"

"Oh, I ran into someone today. He was in my art history program a few years back, and I couldn't stand him. Really self-absorbed. He asked me out a couple of times. Anyway, I guess he got a teaching position here, and he seemed a little too happy to see me. Small world, that's all."

Ben relaxed, exhaling, relieved it wasn't what he'd thought. "That guy, Marshall?"

"Yeah, that's the one. You remember him?"

"I remember. He tried to talk to me about video games." Ben had met him at the Art Department's New Year's party for families. He hadn't liked him any more than his mom had, but the guy had clearly figured it would help his chances with Ben's mom if he made friends with her son.

"I'll just have to do my best to avoid him." She lifted her hand away from her eyes and let her arm fall over the side of the couch. "Shouldn't be too hard. Our departments are across campus from each other."

A little while later, the oven timer dinged. His mom rose from the couch, and they sat down at their table to eat.

The next day, Ben walked past the library twice before going in. The librarian nodded to him over a copy of *The Maltese Falcon* by Dashiell Hammett as he entered and walked past her desk.

"Any good?" he asked.

She winked. "Read it and find out."

He went to the study area, where a few tables were clustered in the middle of the room. Shelves of books surrounded them, and several students huddled together there. Their own little group of outsiders. But Peter wasn't sitting with them. He was at a table by himself, outside the outsiders.

He nodded to Ben, leaning back in his chair, peeling the wrapper back from a granola bar.

"That your lunch?" Ben pulled out the chair opposite him.

"Yes." Half of it disappeared in one bite.

Ben dumped the contents of his brown paper sack on the table. Same as the day before — bologna sandwich with yellow mustard, apple, bottle of water — except there were two bags of chips. One had a note taped to it in his mother's handwriting: *for Peter.* Ben smiled to himself, peeled off the note, and slid the chips across the table. "You want 'em?"

Peter tipped his head at the chips. "Sure. Your mom packs your lunch?"

"Every day." Ben looked at his sandwich. "It's kind of her thing."

"Where does she work?"

"She's in school right now. Getting her master's."

"Oh." Peter opened the bag and ate his chips one at a time, examining each one before popping it into his mouth. "And your dad?"

Ben shook his head. "It's always just been me and her."

Peter nodded.

"What about you?" Ben asked.

"My mom plays the oboe for the city orchestra. My dad teaches economics."

"Do you have any brothers or sisters?"

"A younger sister."

Ben had often thought it'd be nice to have a younger sister. Someone to do the girly stuff with his mom. She was usually pretty good about not asking him that kind of thing, but a sister would be much better for helping her pick outfits.

"So is that why you moved here?" Peter asked. "Your mom's degree?"

"Yeah."

"Where did you move from?"

"Massachusetts."

"Is that where you're from?"

"No. We've lived in lots of places. My mom . . . has a lot going on."

"What do you mean?"

"Just stuff."

"Like what?" Peter ate another chip.

"She just — she has a hard time sticking with anything. This is her second . . . no, I guess it's her third master's. She didn't finish the first one." Ben couldn't even remember the last time he had talked with anyone about this stuff. It felt a little uncomfortable, but there was something about Peter that made Ben feel like he could trust him, so he kept going.

"She's had a million different jobs. It doesn't matter what it is. When she starts something new, I know sooner or later she's going to get bored. So we just keep moving."

"Sorry. Sounds rough."

Ben swallowed. It *was* rough. He just never let himself admit it. "Yeah."

"I actually wish my dad could be more like that."

"What do you mean?"

"Well, he has the opposite problem. He can't let anything go. He has to pin everything down and dissect it."

"Like what?"

"Like me." Peter put down the bag of chips. "I'm a genius."

Wow. Ben hadn't ever heard anyone just come out and say that before. "Okay. Good for you."

"No, really. My dad has had my IQ tested every year since I was six years old."

"Why?"

Peter pushed the bag of chips aside and pointed at the table. "Because he wants to see if it's going up. I'm smart, but he wants me to be smarter. He has me doing all these exercises. The psychologists told him it wouldn't make much of a difference, but he doesn't believe them."

Ben didn't know what to say. "Sorry."

"It's all right." Peter grabbed the edge of the table with both hands and pushed back, balancing on the rear legs of his chair. "He hasn't tested me in a while. I think he's given up on me."

Ben knew his mom had her problems, but one thing she hadn't ever done was make him feel like he wasn't good enough or didn't measure up.

"So, you looking forward to this afternoon?" Peter asked.

"Yeah," Ben said. "But you gotta tell me something."

"What?"

"Did you have anything to do with that cafeteria table?"

Peter paused. "Yes."

"But Dr. Hughes said we can't actuate outside the lab."

Peter smirked. "That's what she told me, too."

"So . . . how did you do it?"

"I don't know," Peter said.

But Ben wondered if that were really true.

That afternoon, Ben actuated a fireball of his own, stoking flame from nothing but the air, and once again, his performance impressed and scared nearly everyone in the room. The ability to do this kind of stuff still bewildered him, but it thrilled him, too. If it were somehow possible to do it outside the lab, in the real world . . . that would be even more incredible.

After his work with Dr. Hughes that day, Ben met his mom at her office. He had to wait for her to finish grading some papers, and by the time she'd finished, the lowering sun had turned everything orange. Their campus apartment wasn't too far, so they decided to walk, but they'd only gone a few paces before someone called to them from behind.

"Heather!"

Ben's mom grimaced. "Oh no." Then she turned around. "Marshall! We have *got* to stop running into each other like this!"

Marshall came trotting up to them. Definitely the same guy as before. But now he had a bit of a gut. "Well, I admit I was hoping to catch you," he said.

His mom smiled with more teeth than usual. "You remember my son, Ben?"

Marshall shook Ben's hand. "Of course. Good to see you again. What was that game you were into? *Viral 3*?"

"*Virus 7*," Ben said.

"Oh, right, right." Marshall bobbed his head enthusiastically, like he was nodding along with a party of people who weren't there. "So, where are you both off to?"

Ben gritted his teeth. *None of your business.*

"Oh, you know." Ben's mom looked away down the sidewalk, their path of escape. "Just heading home. Long day."

"Have you had dinner? Could I take you both out for some pizza? There's a great place just off campus. My treat. Consider it a welcome to the university."

Ben wanted very badly to answer for his mom. But he kept his mouth shut.

"Oh, that's sweet of you, Marshall, but tonight really isn't a good night."

Marshall nodded again, but it had the look of a toy winding down. "Oh. Okay. Some other time, then."

Ben's mom started walking. "But really, thank you for the offer."

"Bye, Heather."

Ben's mom waited until they were well out of earshot. "I don't know how much longer I'll be able to say no politely. I don't want to hurt the man's feelings. He's not a bad guy."

But that didn't mean he was good for Ben's mom.

She sighed. "What do you want to do for dinner?"

"I don't know."

"How about Breakfast Dinner?"

"Sounds good."

They went home and mixed up the pancake batter, fried some eggs and bacon, and then sat down to eat. Ben drenched it all in maple syrup, the real kind he'd gotten used to eating back east. But it got everything sticky, and after they were done eating, he wiped up the table, scouring all the familiar nicks and scratches.

Later that night, as he lay in bed, he thought back to the rain cloud he'd made. And he thought about Dr. Hughes's warning about things getting away from him. A runaway train. He pictured himself back in the basement of the Castle, only this time, the cloud in front of him kept growing and growing, shooting off lightning bolts and booming with thunder. He tried to break it up, to smash the atoms apart with his thoughts. But he couldn't stop its fury.

It took a while to fall asleep after that.

CHAPTER
4

TWO weeks went by. Two weeks of work in Dr. Hughes's lab, where Ben was able to create rain clouds, ignite fires, and move heavy objects, like filing cabinets. Even though Peter didn't make a big deal out of it, Ben knew his friend was secretly bugged that Ben could do stuff Peter couldn't. But Dr. Hughes and the other students continued to be impressed by what Ben could actuate in the lab.

Today, like all the other days, started with a brief lecture on quantum mechanics.

"At the atomic level," Dr. Hughes said, "reality is dependent on our observation of it. As the Nobel-winning physicist Eugene Wigner put it, reality is created when our consciousness 'reaches out.' When you actuate, *you* are reaching out to create a *potential* reality."

Ben shifted in his chair. *Then let's* actuate *something, already.*

"At the atomic level, the world is made of nothing more than possibilities and potentialities. As Actuators, your thoughts guide the world toward a possibility by tipping the scale of probability in one direction or another. So now, let's begin."

Finally!

They worked on ice that day. Snow. Forming it, shaping it, melting it. As he always did, Ben actuated the pants off everyone else, including Peter. And even though that made Dr. Hughes very happy with all the data she was collecting, it left Ben that much more frustrated that he couldn't do something — anything — outside the lab.

As they were wrapping up, and the others were sliding into their backpacks and heading out the door, Dr. Hughes called to Ben.

"Would you mind staying for a moment?"

Ben's mom was studying late that evening, so she wouldn't be expecting him. He looked at Peter, who wore a slight frown. But a moment later, his friend shrugged and left. Ben turned to Dr. Hughes. "Yes?"

"I was wondering if you might assist me with something."

"Sure. What is it?"

From a drawer in her desk, she produced what looked like some kind of gun. As she brought it closer to him, Ben saw that it *was* a gun. A modified laser-tag gun, with a bunch of wires and extra pieces attached to it, including a metal ring almost a foot across mounted at the end of the barrel.

"What's that?" Ben asked.

"The goal of my technology has always been portability. That's where the real excitement will be when I'm ready to share it with the world. This" — she held up the laser-tag gun — "will do the same thing that the augmenting devices have been doing here in the lab. But instead of being confined to a lab, you can take it anywhere. It works directionally. For lack of a better word, you *aim* your thoughts through here" — she pointed at the ring — "and the device will project that thought a certain range."

It wasn't the same as being able to actuate without the technology, like Peter could do, but Ben was still thrilled with the idea of being mobile. "What is the range?"

"Right now, I estimate no more than thirty feet. But it needs to be tested. Which is why you —"

"I'll do it." Ben hadn't meant to sound so eager.

Dr. Hughes grinned. "I thought you might be willing. I've set up a range over here." She led him to a long, narrow stretch of the room she'd cleared of all wires and computers. Little pieces of blue tape marked the distance stretching away from him. "Let's keep doing ice," she said, "since your mind is primed for it."

"Okay."

She handed him the gun. It was heavier than Ben expected, much heavier than the plastic toy it had started out as. He aimed it, looking down the barrel, through the metal ring.

"Let's see the base range without any attempt on your part to control it. Just look through the ring, and actuate a few snowflakes."

"Okay." Ben closed his eyes and, as with rain clouds, he imagined the hydrogen and oxygen atoms in the air coming together. But then he imagined the temperature around the water molecules dropping. That's all he had to do. Lower and lower, to the point of freezing. The water molecules grew very still, and quietly began building themselves into crystalline spears, daggers, arches, petals, and planes. The architecture of ice.

Beside him, Dr. Hughes whispered, "It works."

He opened his eyes. A few feet in front of them, a little pocket of snowflakes floated in the air. Dr. Hughes walked toward it with a clipboard, took some measurements on the floor, and then came back to him.

"Okay, go ahead and melt those. Let's repeat the experiment and see what we get."

Ben was always a little sad about this part. He imagined the temperature rising, and the delicate structure of the snowflakes shattered and collapsed. But then he closed his eyes and actuated the conditions for them to rebuild themselves, which they did. Dr. Hughes took some more measurements, and then he melted them again. They repeated this several times.

"This was an excellent neutral test." Dr. Hughes scanned her notes. "But just for fun, let's try the range on it."

"How do I do that?"

"You'll try to project through the ring, aiming for a distant point. Like raising your voice."

Project.

"Okay. Let me try that."

So he did. He looked through the ring, formed the same thoughts that had been actuating snow for the last thirty minutes, and tried to shout them down the range. Nothing happened. Dr. Hughes offered an encouraging bob of her head, and Ben tried again. He raised his inner voice, yelling his thoughts. His eyes started to water. A quivering started in his shoulders and moved up his neck. Again, nothing.

He lowered the gun, frustrated. "I'm sorry. I don't know why I can't get it to work."

"No need to apologize. I only wish I knew how to give you directions."

"I'm making my thoughts as loud as I can."

Dr. Hughes clicked her pen. "Perhaps it's not about volume," she finally said. "Perhaps it's about tone. And clarity."

"What do you mean?"

"Imagine you're in a stadium. A football game. The roar of the crowd is deafening, and it's impossible to hear a single voice through it all. Right?"

"Right."

"That's the entanglement all around us, filling the universe. There is so much noise, it's impossible for a single voice to be heard. That's the reason actuation isn't happening all the time, with everyone. My technology works by shutting out that noise, isolating and magnifying your individual thoughts."

"So how do I make my thoughts louder than the rest?"

"Not louder. Different. The way a referee's whistle can be heard above the stadium noise."

Ben gripped the gun handle. Not louder. *Different*. "Let me try again."

He raised the barrel, and aimed through the ring, down to the last strip of tape on the floor. He closed his eyes and went through the thoughts to actuate snow. But he stopped screaming them in his head. Instead, he tried to make his thoughts more focused. More clear. Honed like a knife, able to slice through the roaring stadium of entanglement all around him. But he held his thoughts in, like the referee taking a breath before he blew on his whistle.

Then, when he felt ready, Ben opened his eyes and released the actuation.

A jagged shard of ice the size of a football exploded from the air in front of him. It shot down the range, past the last tape marker, and shattered against the wall.

Ben was stunned.

Dr. Hughes stared.

"What was that?" Ben asked with an excited laugh.

She blinked. "I have no idea. Is that what you meant to actuate?"

"No. I was still going for snow. But I was also thinking about what you said, and I was trying to focus my thoughts."

"You're certain that is not what you intended?"

"I swear."

"Nothing in my calculations predicted something like this. That could have been dangerous. I —" She paused. "In the interest of safety, I need to revisit the data before we use the portable augmenter again." She held out her hand.

Ben gave her the gun, a little reluctant to let it go.

"Thank you for your work today," she said. "See you tomorrow afternoon."

"Sorry," Ben said, even though he didn't feel sorry. He wanted to try the gun again. "See you tomorrow, Dr. Hughes."

On his way home, Ben kept his hands in his pockets, watching the sidewalk seams pass underfoot. How had he done that? Made a missile of ice. What else could he do? What were the limits of his power?

He looked up at the sky, wondering whether he should tell Peter what he had done. Probably not. Dr. Hughes hadn't specifically asked him to keep it a secret, but Ben figured she wouldn't want him going around telling everyone else about the augmenter gun that let you shoot ice cannonballs. The gray clouds overhead looked like they might rain. They reminded Ben of his first actuation.

He stopped.

Could he do it without the lab equipment? Now that he had figured out how to project his thoughts, how to rise above the noise, maybe he could do what Peter had done that day in the cafeteria. Maybe Ben could make things happen outside the lab.

He studied the cloud. He thought about where it would rain, and how it would rain, and how the water would patter the trees, and flow down the gutters. He thought about the smell, and the way the grass would get slick. He imagined a warm updraft lifting humid air into the heart of the cloud, where the molecules in the water vapor bumped and gathered together, forming droplets. And then he imagined these droplets getting big enough that gravity got ahold of them and brought them falling down.

This was a lot bigger than flipping a penny or closing a cafeteria table. But he sent this thought out, an actuation, just as he had with the augmenter gun.

Then he watched and waited. It seemed like it maybe got a little more windy. But no rain fell. Nothing happened.

CHAPTER 5

"I thought he stopped having you tested." Ben sat next to Peter on the bus, heading up to the university.

Peter's expression and voice came out flat. "I did, too."

Ben watched the wavering threads of water stretching across the bus window. The storm had eventually started up this morning. *Un*-actuated. "So. When do you go in?"

Peter shrugged with one shoulder. "This Saturday. I'm considering bombing this one on purpose. Maybe the man just needs a sign to give up hope."

"Don't bomb it."

"Why not? It's up to me."

"Yeah, but . . . what your dad does isn't up to you."

Peter fell silent. The bus chugged along and soon arrived at the campus. By the time they reached the basement of the Castle, they were both drenched. But so were the other students, who were all dripping outside in the hallway. The classroom door was closed and locked.

"Where is Dr. Hughes?" Ben asked.

"Dunno." Dylan handed Ben a piece of paper. "This was taped to the door."

Ben read the note: *Class, I will be late for our session today. Please feel free to take the afternoon off, if you do not want to wait for me. If you do wait, I hope I won't be long.*

"So she's coming," Ben said.

Abbie shrugged. "Guess so."

"I think I'm gonna go," Julie said. "Bye, guys." And she left.

Ten minutes later, Dylan and Abbie left, too. Ben sat down on the floor, his back against the wall, legs outstretched. Peter sat against the wall opposite him, his legs crossed. He kept looking at his watch, and Ben figured he probably wanted to leave, but he wasn't going to if Ben was staying. And Ben planned to wait. It was either here for Dr. Hughes, or somewhere else for his mom.

A short while later, Dr. Hughes strode down the hallway, pumping the water off a blue umbrella, a slim package tucked under her arm.

"Ben! Peter! Sorry I'm late. Did the others leave?"

"Yes," Peter said.

"That's too bad. I have exciting news."

"What is it?" Ben asked.

She pulled out her keys and unlocked the classroom door. "Let's talk about it inside."

The fluorescent lights flickered on down the length of the room with a buzzing sound. The gun range he'd used the day before was gone. Dr. Hughes went to her desk and set the package down, while Ben and Peter took two chairs nearby.

"I apologize for my tardiness," she said. "But I think you'll find your patience rewarded."

Ben and Peter waited.

Dr. Hughes came over and sat down near them in one of the other chairs. "I am not the first to have explored and experimented with actuation. There are others, though I don't know their real names, but I doubt any have come as far as I have."

"What others?" Ben asked. "And why don't you know their names?"

"They're physicists like myself. Professors. Government researchers. People whose professional reputations could suffer if our interests in quantum actuation were made public. We've formed a loose network, using pseudonyms. Well, after yesterday's" — Dr. Hughes looked at Ben, and then seemed to remember that Peter was sitting there — "unpredicted results, I contacted a man I've been in touch with for several months to get his input on portable augmentation."

"Portable?" Peter looked back and forth between Ben and Dr. Hughes. "What do you mean, portable?"

"In a moment, Peter." Dr. Hughes straightened in her chair. "This man . . . oh, what name did he go by? That's funny, I'm normally good with names." She tapped her lips with her index finger. "Richter! That was it. At any rate, this man got back to me, and it turns out he's been interested in portable augmentation as well. We agreed to share some results, and he overnighted me a package with copies of his work. I've been glancing through it, and I believe he'll be a useful research ally going forward."

An ally. What had she said his name was? Ben had already forgotten. Something . . . Richter? Yes, Richter. That was it.

"So what did you mean by portable augmentation?" Peter asked.

Dr. Hughes folded her hands in her lap. "Well, it's something I've been working on from the beginning, the end goal, actually. Yesterday, I asked Ben to stay and help me with it. But we did not get the results I was expecting, and that caused me a bit of alarm. We must make certain that at each step we take every precaution."

Ben wondered if Peter would be bothered, knowing Dr. Hughes had picked Ben instead of him.

Peter said, "And this man who sent you the package . . . what was his name?"

Dr. Hughes blinked. "Um."

"Richter," Ben said. *Richter.* Something about the name felt slippery in his mind.

"Yes," Dr. Hughes said. "Richter."

"Right," Peter said. "So this man might be able to help you with portable augmentation?"

"That is my hope," Dr. Hughes said.

"Can I try it?" Peter asked.

Dr. Hughes sighed. "I don't think so. Not yet, anyway. I have to make sure it's working as predicted by the math."

Peter hitched his frown to one side. "Okay."

"So that was the exciting news?" Ben asked.

"Yes!" she said. "Don't you find it exciting?"

"Yeah. Sure." But the gun still didn't quite work yet.

They spent the rest of the afternoon back at what had now become routine for Ben, with the standard equipment in the actuation rings. After wielding the augmenter gun, and creating a missile of ice, conjuring a little rain cloud just didn't hold the same appeal. Still, the afternoon passed pretty smoothly with the other kids gone.

Ben and Peter even started playing off each other in the actuation ring. Ben would actuate snow, and Peter would actuate a little flame to melt it. Then Ben would actuate a rain cloud, and Peter would turn it into snow. It felt a bit like chess. Or a duel.

"Let's wrap up for today, gentlemen," Dr. Hughes finally said.

Ben and Peter nodded to each other, let go of their actuations, and went to collect their things.

"I'll be looking through the notes from . . ." Dr. Hughes snapped her fingers by her ear.

Ben reached for the name, and just barely found it. *Richter.*

"Um . . . him." Dr. Hughes flicked her hand away. "Anyway, our new ally, after which I hope to have some idea of how to proceed with the portable augmenter. With luck, you'll be able to try it soon, Peter."

"I look forward to that, Dr. —"

A deafening boom, and the door to the lab blew inward off its hinges. It flew across the room and slammed into several of the tripods. Sparks scattered across the floor where they fell. A swarm of men wearing black ski masks spilled through the smoking doorway.

Dr. Hughes gasped. Peter yelled something. Ben's thoughts went to defense. To ice. To actuation. But fear scattered his thoughts before they could form, let alone reach out to make anything. And then two of the men grabbed him and held him by the arms.

"What is this?" Dr. Hughes cried out. "Who are you?"

The intruders had her, too, and Peter. Who they were didn't matter right now. Ben had to do something. If he could somehow get into one of the actuation areas, then he might be able to.

One of the men swaggered forward. "We're the Dread Cloaks. So best beware." His voice came out hoarse, and as well as the ski masks, he and the others all wore the same clothing. Polished black boots, black pants, and black vests over bloodred dress shirts. "You have something we want."

Dr. Hughes thrashed but couldn't break free. "What could I possibly have?"

The man's shrouded gaze roamed from one side of the room to the other. "A portable augmenter. That's what you called it, right?"

"What? How do you —?"

He made a sweeping gesture with his arm, and one of the computers nearby leaped from its desk and smashed into pieces against a wall several yards away.

Ben knew actuation when he saw it. He could feel it. These were no simple robbers, or terrorists, or anything like that. And the man had actuated without any augmenting equipment at all. Ben looked at Peter, but his friend just stared wide-eyed at the floor. Was he in shock?

"You . . ." Dr. Hughes whispered. "Who do you work for? Who sent you?"

"You insult us," the man said. "The Dread Cloaks are not for hire. Now where is it?"

Dr. Hughes looked so small, her eyes so big. She began to shake.

"How about I do to one of these boys like I just did to your computer?" The man held up his arm like he was preparing to backhand something — or someone.

Ben swallowed. Would it be him or Peter? Ben was about

a foot away from one of the actuation rings. If he could just step inside it, he could summon something. But what? A little cloud? What would that do? No, he needed something powerful. An ice missile. A fireball. A lightning bolt. He tried to make eye contact with Peter, but his friend was still looking downward.

"Don't harm them!" Dr. Hughes cried. "Let them go, and I'll tell you where it is."

The man brought his arm down. "Show me where it is, and I might not kill them."

Dr. Hughes bit her lip, still shaking. "In my desk. It's just over there in my desk."

The man flicked his head, and one of the others crossed the room. He pulled each of the drawers open, and a moment later came back with the augmenter gun in his hand. He passed it to his leader, who brandished it in front of Dr. Hughes.

"This? This is it?"

Dr. Hughes nodded. "Now let them go."

The man studied the device in his hand. "Show me how it works."

"It doesn't," Dr. Hughes said. "Not reliably."

"Show me!" His hoarse voice became a tortured growl.

Ben felt the grip on his arms relax a little. His captors had become distracted by the augmenter gun. He closed his eyes and started gathering his thoughts. Calming his breathing. A lightning bolt. He would summon a lightning bolt. He pictured the oxygen atoms in front of him; he imagined a disturbance in the air, bouncing the atoms off one another, knocking electrons loose. He gathered these electrons in front of him, charging them up. He held them there, and opened his eyes.

Dr. Hughes was pointing at something on the augmenter gun in the Dread Cloak leader's hand. Everyone in the room was looking. Now was his chance.

Ben yanked his arms free and leaped backward into the circle. He focused on the nearest Dread Cloak and, without thinking, let the actuation go with a single clap of his hands in front of him.

A searing arc of light shot forward and struck the Dread Cloak in the chest. He bolted upright onto his toes, stiff, and then collapsed to the ground. Ben closed his eyes to try to summon another, but the attackers were on him instantly.

"Get him out of there!" their leader shouted. "And make sure Riggs is still alive."

Ben fought and kicked and wriggled, but he couldn't break free. Two men dragged him from the circle, across the floor, and forced him to his knees next to Dr. Hughes.

The leader bent down close. Ben could see his eyes were blue through the slits in the ski mask. "Hello, hero boy. That was a devilish trick. Care to try it on me?"

"Too easy," Ben said.

"Defiance. I like that." The leader stood and looked back at the man Ben had struck. "Well?"

"He's alive," came the reply. "He's coming around."

The Dread Cloak leader returned his focus to Ben. "A fine little playpen you have here, with your toys. But you've just toddled into the grown-up world, and I think you will find it a painful place."

"Don't hurt him," Dr. Hughes said. "Please. I beg you."

"Leave him alone!" Peter shouted.

Ben looked at his friend. Something had finally roused him.

"We have two hero boys?" The leader coughed. "Bring him here."

They hauled Peter over and threw him down next to Ben.

Dr. Hughes tried to lean toward them. "I'm sorry, boys, I —"

"Silence, Doctor." The leader looked around the room. "Quite clever to have built all of this. But in the end, of what use is it?" He held up the augmenter gun. "But this. This I can make terrible use of."

"I told you, it doesn't work reliably!"

"Then I will need you to continue working on it." The leader turned to Ben. "But devilish children must not be left to run amok. Kill the boys."

CHAPTER
6

BEN'S mind burned hot, but gave him nothing. He looked at Peter. He looked at Dr. Hughes. What could he do? He had never actuated without any equipment. He didn't think he could do it now, but he closed his eyes to try for another lightning bolt.

"None of that, hero boy!"

Something knocked the side of his head. Hard. Ben felt a sharp pain, and the actuation broke apart in his mind with a shower of sparks.

"How should we do it?" one of the Dread Cloaks asked.

Their leader paused. "I have an idea. Take them over there." He pointed at a spot on the ground several feet away.

The Dread Cloaks holding them shoved Ben and Peter across the floor to the spot, then let go of them and backed away.

Ben looked at the doorway. It wasn't too far. His head throbbed, and he closed his eyes. He couldn't think straight. He considered running, but couldn't bring himself to leave Peter and Dr. Hughes.

"You say this device doesn't work, Doctor." The Dread Cloak leader aimed the augmenter gun at Ben. "So you must be perfectly comfortable with me doing this."

"Please, don't." She held out both hands. "I said it was unreliable."

Ben looked straight through the metal ring at the end of the gun.

"Well, let's just see what it does," the leader said. "Unreliably."

Ben thought of his mom, not too far away, on the other side of campus. She wouldn't know what had happened to him.

"They're here!" A Dread Cloak ran into the lab. "The League has come!"

"Bring her!" The leader pointed at Dr. Hughes. "And make a door!" He looked back at Ben, still aiming the gun.

Ben felt a . . . disturbance. The beginning of an actuation coming through the ring. He knew something bad was about to happen to him. But in that moment, a troop of uniformed people charged into the lab through the broken doorway.

"Drop the weapon, Poole!" one of them shouted.

The Dread Cloak leader held up his hands. "You think you've caught me?"

An explosion at the far end of the lab threw Ben to the floor. The impact struck the core of his chest and blew out his hearing. It was dark now, the room filling with smoke. He rolled onto his back. Wires hung from the gaping ceiling, and the walls bloomed fire. People rushed around him. He saw Peter lying on the ground beside him.

Then he didn't see anything at all.

When Ben woke up, he was lying on a cot in a white room. White walls, white ceiling tiles, white linoleum floor. Was he in a hospital? Peter lay on a cot next to him. He was sleeping, but he didn't look hurt. Ben sat up, and felt a pain stab his temple. He reached his hand up to it, and found a bandage. It must be a hospital. But when he went to the door, he found it locked.

He knocked. "Hello? Is anyone there?"

"Ben?" Peter had woken up. "Where are we?"

"I don't know," Ben said. "You okay?"

"Yes, I think so." Peter rubbed his hair. "My head hurts."

"Mine, too." But it was more than that. He felt disoriented, like he was floating, and not in a good way. More like he was getting pulled out to sea.

Something clicked in the door, and Ben stepped back as it opened. Two people walked in, a man and a woman, both wearing suits. Their faces looked familiar, and then Ben remembered seeing them back in Dr. Hughes's lab. They were part of the second group that came in after the Dread Cloaks. Who were they? Cops? Military?

"Ben, Peter." The man was tall and lanky, and carried a manila file in his hand. "I'm Agent Spear. This is Agent Taggart." He spoke with a slight southern accent.

The woman nodded. She had red hair and lots of freckles. "We're relieved you weren't seriously injured."

Agents? What did that mean? FBI?

"Where are we?" Ben asked. "Where is Dr. Hughes?"

"Have a seat." Agent Spear pointed at the cot with the file he held. "Let's talk."

Ben and Peter both hesitated, but sat down side by side on Peter's cot. Agent Spear sat down on the low cot across from them, his knees almost bumping his chin, while Agent Taggart stood back by the door, arms folded. Spear opened the file and began to read over whatever was in there, licking his thumb and turning pages. A few moments later, he looked up and smiled.

"Right. You boys have stepped in it now, haven't you?"

"Stepped in what?" Peter asked.

"The battlefield. The Quantum War."

"War?" Ben asked.

"Well, I don't mean a war between nations," Agent Spear said. "It's a street war. A gang war."

"Who are you?" Ben asked. "And where's Dr. Hughes?"

"We belong to an agency," Spear said. "You could think of it like other intelligence agencies you might be more familiar with, but we don't answer to any government. We're the Quantum League. Agent Taggart and I are Quantum Agents."

Peter cocked his head. "What *is* the Quantum League? What do you do?"

"Our agency has tasked itself with —"

"Where is Dr. Hughes?" Ben raised his voice. "This is the third time we've asked." It seemed like there was something this Agent Spear didn't want to tell them.

Peter leaned back a bit on the cot, silenced.

Agent Spear sighed. "Okay. You demand the truth, and I'll give it to you straight. We don't know where Dr. Hughes is. The Dread Cloaks abducted her when they made their escape. She could be in any one of their hideouts."

"Can you rescue her?" Ben asked.

Agent Taggart spoke up from the door. "A direct frontal assault against the Dread Cloaks would not be in our strategic interests."

"What she means," Agent Spear said, "is that we don't have the firepower to take on the whole gang."

"Whole gang?" Peter asked. "How many are there?"

"Current estimates," Agent Taggart said, "put their membership between three and five hundred."

The number shocked Ben, and at first he wasn't sure he had heard it right. Between three and five *hundred*? And how many of those were Actuators? Would they hurt Dr.

Hughes? Was she alive? Each question hit Ben's head like a hammer strike. He felt disoriented, his world all ground up. Just weeks ago he'd learned about actuation, and then the lab was attacked by a gang, and now this skinny guy was calling himself an agent and talking about a war.

Ben still felt adrift, and the waves were starting to break over his head. "I'd like to call my mom now."

"That's been taken care of," Agent Spear said. "You needn't worry."

"What does that mean?" Ben asked. "Let me call my mom."

Agent Spear closed the folder. He looked over his shoulder at Agent Taggart, who checked something on a small device she pulled from her pocket. She gave him a nod back.

Agent Spear stood. "Let me show you boys something."

"What?" Peter asked.

Ben stayed seated. "I don't want to see anything. I'm not going anywhere. I want a phone."

Agent Spear looked around. "You see one in here, son?"

Peter tugged on his sleeve. "Come on, Ben."

Ben looked hard at Agent Spear. The man met his gaze with the kind of smile fathers gave their boys in commercials. "Things will make sense again real soon. I promise." He walked to the door and grasped the handle. "Coming?"

Ben looked at Peter. His friend bounced a little as he nodded. Ben got to his feet. The two of them crossed the room, and as they approached the door, Agent Spear opened it.

They entered into a hallway that felt a little like the Castle back at the university. Old. White walls, smoky wood trim.

"Right this way, gentlemen," Agent Taggart said.

She led the way, while Agent Spear came behind them. They followed the hallway, turned a couple of corners, and stopped before another door.

"This is the training room." Agent Taggart pressed a button, and a loud buzzer sounded before she opened the door.

They entered into a huge vaulted room. Areas of the floor had been sectioned off by partial walls of different materials. The nearest one was made of cinder block, and it bore blackened scorch marks and craters across its surface.

The people inside, some of them as young as Ben and Peter, had stopped whatever they'd been doing and stared as Agent Taggart led them through the room. Some wore protective armor, like they were on a bomb squad. Others wore heavy padding that made them look puffy and stiff. The rest of the people either wore plain workout clothes, or suits like Agent Spear and Agent Taggart. Ben made eye contact with a girl who looked a few years older than him. She had long black hair, shiny and smooth as electrical tape, with a single lock dyed bright blue.

When they reached the far side of the room, Agent Taggart spun around.

"What kind of training are they doing?" Peter asked.

"Watch," Agent Taggart said. "It should look familiar to you." She cupped her hand to her mouth. "Clear!"

The room resumed motion. People took up positions. Ben felt something change in the air. Then fireballs flew. Ice. Lightning. Blasts of wind. The girl with the black-blue hair smirked at Ben before launching a baseball-sized rock from a pile into the air like a bullet. Ben glanced at Peter, whose wide eyes and open mouth looked how Ben felt. *Actuation.* This was an actuation training room.

Except, Ben didn't see any augmenting equipment. He looked around, along the walls, up into the heavy timber rafters that stretched across the ceiling. Nothing. It seemed that every person in that room was actuating on his or her own.

Agent Taggart waited a moment longer, and then motioned for Ben and Peter to follow her through another door. Ben didn't want to leave. Peter didn't move, either. He just stared. But Agent Spear shepherded them forward, and they soon stood in a quiet hallway.

"Quantum Agents," Peter whispered. "Now it makes sense. But —"

"Let's finish this in the library." Agent Spear took the lead again, and they followed him down a few more turns into a room that was smaller than the one they'd just been in, but larger than the room where they'd started. Empty wooden shelves lined the walls — was it still a library if it didn't have any books? — and a couple of conference tables rested in the middle of the room, surrounded by high-backed wooden chairs. They each took a seat.

"What is this place?" Ben asked.

"It used to be a church," Agent Spear said. "They were going to tear it down, but the League moved in before they could."

"So this is your headquarters?" Peter asked.

"One of them," Agent Taggart said. "The League is a global agency. We monitor quantum activity around the world and make sure groups like the Dread Cloaks don't get too powerful or cause too much trouble. We stop them when we can."

Ben thought back to what the leader of the Dread Cloaks had done to the computer in Dr. Hughes's lab. "Can they all . . . well, Dr. Hughes called it actuation?"

Agent Taggart nodded. "That is the scientific term we use as well. Although, you may occasionally hear an older agent still calling it magic. But that's usually as a joke. As for the Dread Cloaks, yes. Most of them can actuate, to varying degrees."

"Does the government know about them?" Ben asked. "Or, you guys?"

"No," Agent Spear said.

"How is that possible?" Peter asked.

"That's the funny thing about actuation," Agent Spear said. "Ennays have a hard time seeing it."

"Ennays?" Ben asked.

"Non-Actuators," Agent Taggart said. "N-A's. Most people who cannot actuate don't really perceive it. It is a part of reality they are blind to, just like you're blind to infrared light. They see the aftermath of actuation, but they attribute it to other things. Freak storms. Freak accidents. Spontaneous combustion. That kind of thing."

"Another term for Ennays you might hear is Imps," Agent Spear said. "Short for *impotent*. Powerless. But that's an insult, so don't go picking it up."

But Ben thought back to how Dr. Hughes had trained them. "If Dr. Hughes is an Ennay, how does *she* see it?"

"Her equipment allows her to perceive it," Agent Taggart said. "Like you wearing infrared goggles."

"Which brings us back to the attack," Agent Spear said. "Poole is in charge of the Dread Cloaks, and for him to personally head up an operation means there was something very important in that lab. And with Dr. Hughes."

Agent Spear scratched absently with a fingernail at the deep grain of the table. "You boys know what that might be?"

"They wanted her portable augmenter," Peter said.

"Portable?" Agent Taggart's voice turned sharp. "Was it functional?"

"I don't know, I didn't . . ." Peter turned to Ben.

So did both agents.

Ben leaned back. "I used it. It worked . . . kind of. But Dr. Hughes said it wasn't reliable. I think that's why Poole took her."

"You're *certain* it worked?" Agent Taggart asked.

"Yeah."

She whipped out her phone, stabbed at the screen, and as she got up she lifted it to her ear. "This is Taggart. Put me through to Mr. Weathersky." She left the room.

Ben was confused. "What's the big —"

"Augmentation can be extremely dangerous," Agent Spear said. "The one thing that's kept us all safe from it is that it's theoretically impossible to make the technology mobile. Until now, apparently."

That didn't make sense. Augmentation was a crutch. No one in that training room had seemed to need it. "Why would it be dangerous?" Ben asked.

Agent Spear's forehead wrinkled. "I can see Dr. Hughes got a few things wrong with you boys. So let me break this down for you. Actuation is not about the technology. It's about you, the Actuator, and it has limits. You can only get so big before the whole thing falls apart in your mind. You've got your Class One actuations. Those would be, say, moving small objects. Then you've got your Class Two actuations, the most common. That's what you saw in the training room. Or like what Poole did to escape, when he triggered that explosion in the gas line. Class Three actuations are much bigger, extremely difficult, and rarely attempted."

"Like what?" Peter asked.

"A Class Three is a Class Two on a larger scale. It affects a whole system. Instead of a little Class Two cloud, you get a full storm, maybe even a tornado or hurricane. Change the weather."

"Is there a Class Four?" Peter asked.

Agent Spear chuckled. "*Theoretically*, there are Class Four and even Class Five actuations. But they only work on paper, not in real life. No one in recorded history has brought one about."

"What would those even be?" Ben asked.

"A Class Four? Maybe an earthquake. A Class Five? I can't even imagine. The point is, most Actuators can only accomplish Class One and Two. Very, very few can hit a Three. Without augmentation."

Now it was starting to make sense to Ben. Poole had wanted the augmenter because it had the potential to make him even more powerful. And while the stationary laboratory imposed limits on what could be actuated, portability made the technology a formidable weapon.

"So what happens now?" Ben asked.

"Now?" Agent Spear looked back and forth between Ben and Peter. "Now is the part where I ask you boys to join the Quantum League."

CHAPTER
7

BEN knew he had seen people not much older than him in the training room, but still. Joining the Quantum League? "Um. I'm twelve."

"I'll be thirteen next month," Peter said.

"You're both in the target range," Agent Spear said. "Ideal recruitment age is between eight and fourteen. But we usually don't go as young as eight. Beyond fourteen, you start to think you know what's going on in the world, and it just gets worse with age."

"But you're an adult," Ben said.

Agent Spear aimed a crooked smile at the table. "I joined when I was ten. I believe Agent Taggart was thirteen. That's the way it works."

"What about your parents?" Peter asked. "They must have —"

"Got along just fine without me." Agent Spear's voice turned suddenly curt. "As will yours."

Ben did not like how that sounded. His body went cold, and the disorientation returned. "I'd like to call my mom now."

Agent Spear didn't respond.

Ben raised his voice. "You said I could call my mom!"

Agent Spear sighed. "If you look back at my words carefully, I think you'll find I said no such thing."

Ben felt a panic rising he couldn't control. "I don't care. Let me call my mom. Now!"

The warmth returned to the agent's voice. "Calm down, son. You need to listen to me carefully. What I'm about to tell you will be hard, but I promise you'll get through it. Every agent has gone through the same process. It's just the way of things."

Ben stood. "I'm not listening anymore. I'm leaving."

Peter grabbed his arm. "Ben, don't."

Ben looked down at his friend. Somehow, Peter didn't seem bothered by any of this. In fact, he looked excited.

"Just hear him out," Peter said. "Before you walk away."

Ben snatched his arm free. "But this is kidnapping."

"You have not been kidnapped," Agent Spear said. "You are free to leave if you so choose. But you do need to hear me out first."

"No, I don't." Ben went for the door. "I'm leaving now."

"She won't know you."

Ben stopped. He turned around. Agent Spear had risen to his feet.

"What?"

"She won't know you."

Ben swallowed. "What do you mean?"

"Please, come sit down."

"TELL ME WHAT YOU MEAN!" Ben held both his hands in fists.

Agent Spear's voice remained calm, his face gentle. "You have been detached, Ben. So have you, Peter."

"What does that mean?" Peter remained in his chair.

"It means that the previous connections to your lives have been severed. For your families, your teachers, your friends, it will be like you never existed."

Ben's stomach felt like it was grinding up ice cubes, and a smothering dread settled over him. He couldn't find any words. He couldn't breathe.

Agent Spear continued. "We performed the procedure while you were unconscious in the holding room. Believe me when I say it was absolutely necessary."

"Why?" Peter asked.

Ben couldn't understand how his friend was dealing with this so calmly.

"To be blunt," Agent Spear said, "because you're kids. Very few parents would just up and agree to let their kids go. This is the easiest way for you, and for them."

But Ben didn't really care about himself. What would his mom do without him? She needed him. Who would help her? Who would remind her to take her pills? He felt tears rising, a tightening in his throat, but he coughed and kept it under control. Now was not the time to lose it.

"I don't want to be an agent," Ben said. "Put me back. Re . . . reattach me."

The door opened behind him, and Agent Taggart came back into the room. She saw Ben, looked past him to Agent Spear, and nodded. "Ah. You told them."

"Reattach me," Ben said to both of them.

"I'm afraid we can't do that." Agent Taggart held up her phone. "Mr. Weathersky is on his way."

"He's coming here?" Agent Spear asked.

"Yes. And until this matter is resolved, he feels that we may have further need of you gentlemen." She looked down at Ben. "I'm afraid you don't have a choice. This is no longer an invitation to join the League. You've been drafted."

Ben narrowed his eyes at her. "I don't think so. You can't do this." He pushed past her out the door.

"Ben!" Peter shouted.

"Let him go," Agent Spear said. "He needs to . . ."

But Ben didn't stick around to hear the rest. He started down the hallway, took a turn, then another. This place used to be a church, not a maze. He had to find a way out, eventually. And soon, he did. It was an emergency exit, with one of those big red alarm levers. Ben didn't care. He shouldered it open, hard, and took the cement staircase outside three steps down at a time, while a siren blared behind him. He looked back up at the building. It really had been a church, with white siding and a single square steeple.

It had also quit raining. Ben looked down the street, saw a bus approaching a stop, and took off running toward it.

"Mom!" He raced toward her office. He knew her schedule; she wasn't in class right now, so hopefully, he'd find her there. She *would* remember him. She had to remember him. He knocked on the door, and then opened it. "Mom?"

She swiveled around from her computer to face him. He looked in her eyes. She looked back, and he could see it. Clearly. She didn't know him.

"Can I help you?" she asked.

This wasn't possible. This could not be happening. He hadn't believed Agent Spear when he'd said she wouldn't know him. But now that he'd seen it for himself, it felt like something had broken loose inside him, something jagged and sharp, migrating around in his chest. He couldn't help it, he started crying.

"Oh, I'm so sorry." She got up and came over to him. "Here, what is it, who are you looking for? Let me help you find them."

He shook his head. He swiped at his tears with his sleeve and got himself back under control, even though the pain was still slicing through him. "I'm okay," he said. "I'm fine."

"Are you sure?" She looked at the bandage on his head. "What happened to you?"

It was her. Her eyes. Her nose. Her smile. But he wasn't him, not to her.

"It's nothing. I'm fine," he said. "Ha-have we ever met before?"

"Hmm. I don't think so. Is your mother another teaching assistant? Or a professor?"

"Teaching assistant. But I think I got the wrong office."

"Do you want me to help you find her?"

"No." He pulled away. And that hurt, too. "No, I'll just call her."

"All right. But come back if you can't find her."

"Okay, thanks."

"Wait. Before you go, what's your name?"

"Ben," he said, his own name catching in his throat.

"And what's your mom's name?"

He hesitated. "Heather."

"Really?" She smiled. "What a coincidence! That's my name. If she works in this building, maybe I'll run into her sometime."

"Maybe you will," Ben said.

He left, and he could feel her watching him stumble down the hallway. Once he reached the elevator, she gave him a little wave and went back into her office. He pushed the down button, and ended up on the first floor without even remembering the elevator ride. Maybe she just needed time. Time to recover from whatever they'd done to her. To him.

Outside on the street, he turned toward home. He'd go and wait there, and see how she reacted when she saw him in their apartment. She'd either be normal about it, or he'd really freak her out. Either way, he had to try.

He passed a campus newspaper someone had left on a bench, and the cover headline caught his eye. It was a story about a gas explosion in the basement of the Castle. No one was hurt, the article explained, but the building was old, and discussions were under way about whether to tear it down or renovate it. The article also mentioned that Professor Madeleine Hughes of the Physics Department, whose lab was at the epicenter of the blast, had been missing since the accident, but that she was not believed to have been present at the time. No mention of him or Peter.

Ben threw the paper in the trash and kept walking.

He reached their apartment a short while later, but found Agent Spear leaning against the door like a tree.

"What are you doing here?" Ben shoved past him to get to the lock. "I could call the cops."

Agent Spear stepped aside. "You could. But that won't end well for anyone, including you. How will you feel when your mom denies you're her son to the police? What'll happen to you then? The cops will take you, they won't be able to find your parents, and you'll go into the foster system."

Ben pressed his forehead against the door. "This is insane." He squeezed his eyes shut, and punched the door hard. "Why are you doing this to me? She needs me!"

"Not anymore, son." Agent Spear put a hand on Ben's back. "She never knew you."

"But she's here." He thrashed the agent's hand away. "If she never knew me, how come she's still here and everything is the same?"

"Detachment doesn't undo cause and effect. It just breaks the connection of her consciousness and yours."

"But I remember her."

"And you always will, I'm afraid."

Ben clenched his jaw. The pain was still there. He wanted to scream. "Just give me my life back. Please."

"Okay."

Okay?

Ben turned to Agent Spear.

"These are special circumstances," the man said. "And we need you. You're the only one who's used the portable augmenter. You help us recover it, and we'll restore your life." He extended a hand. "Deal?"

"Restore it now, and then I'll help you."

Agent Spear shook his head. "Afraid I can't do that. This mission might take days or even weeks. We can't have your mom going stir-crazy missing you and looking for you that whole time." He still held out his hand. "You don't want to cause her that pain, do you?"

Ben thought back to the way his mom had looked at him. No recognition. No familiarity. It had made him feel like he wasn't himself. But maybe it was better this way for her. "After the mission, you'll put things back. She'll know me again."

"You'll have your life back."

"You swear?"

"I swear."

"Peter, too?"

"If that's what Peter wants. But that's *his* decision."

Ben eyed the agent's hand for a long moment. And then he shook it.

Back at the Quantum League headquarters, Peter greeted Ben with a broad grin. "Glad you came back."

Ben couldn't say the same, but he was at least glad to see Peter again. "You were pretty eager to join up."

Peter spread his arms wide. "Why wouldn't I be? Now my dad won't have to worry about whether I'm smart enough."

"What about your mom and your sister?"

"They won't know what they're missing."

"But won't you?"

Peter shrugged. "I'll get over it."

"Just like that?"

"Just like that."

Maybe Peter could do that. Ben couldn't. But then, he didn't have a home like Peter did. Maybe things would actually be better for his friend here, a fresh start with the Quantum League. Maybe this was where Peter belonged. But what would happen to Peter after the mission was over, and Ben left to go home?

"Gentlemen," Agent Taggart said. "It's time to get you two squared away, and then I'll introduce you to your trainer."

Ben and Peter followed her to a supply room, where she loaded their arms with black uniforms, sheets, and gray wool blankets. After that, she led them downstairs into the basement. It was a large single room with a low ceiling, and it smelled like popcorn. White square columns marched down the basement's center. There was a sitting area around a large TV, and an old, wrinkled pool table. Ben figured the space had probably been used by the church's youth program, but now served as the barracks. Metal-framed beds lined the walls on either side. Agent Taggart led them down the rows to two beds at the far end.

"These will be yours," she said. "Men are downstairs, women are upstairs."

"Okay," Ben said.

"Drop your things," she said. "You can make your beds later."

Ben and Peter dumped their stuff on their beds and followed Agent Taggart back upstairs. They went to the training room, and in spite of his resistance to being in the League,

Ben took an excited step toward the door as Agent Taggart pressed the buzzer.

They went inside, and just like before, all the actuation had stopped.

Agent Taggart checked something on her phone. "I need Agent Lambert, please!"

The girl Ben had seen earlier, the one with the blue-and-black hair, came toward them, and Agent Taggart ushered the three of them back out into the hall.

"Yes?" the girl said, eyeing Ben and Peter sideways.

"Agent Lambert, these are our newest recruits. Just detached today."

"Welcome." She smiled.

"This is Ben, and this is Peter. They were with Dr. Hughes at the university."

"That class we've had under surveillance?" Agent Lambert asked.

"Yes," Agent Taggart said. "So they've had some rudimentary training. I'm entrusting you to pick up where Dr. Hughes left off, and fix any mistakes she may have made."

It bothered Ben to think that the League had been spying on their science camp. Like the detaching, and the drafting, the League seemed to think it could do whatever it wanted.

Agent Lambert nodded. "Understood."

Agent Taggart checked her phone again. "And now if you'll excuse me, I must go prepare for Mr. Weathersky."

"He's coming here?" Agent Lambert seemed to react with the same surprise that Agent Spear had.

"Yes. He'll arrive early tomorrow. Now get to work." With that, Agent Taggart left.

Agent Lambert watched her until she'd rounded a corner, and then she turned to Ben and Peter. "Okay, when there aren't any agents around, call me Sasha."

"But . . ." Peter said. "Aren't you an agent?"

"Junior agent. I'm more like you than them." She tucked her hair behind her ears. "But when it comes to actuation, I'm better than any of them. Which is why they have me training you two."

This girl had an even bigger ego than Peter. "Who is Mr. Weathersky?"

"He's the head of the Quantum League's North American Division." Sasha tipped her head. "He's also one of the few men on the planet who can handle Class Three actuations. You know what *that* means, right?"

"Agent Spear explained it," Peter said.

Sasha nodded. "I like Spear. A lot more than Taggart."

"Does Mr. Weathersky come here often?"

"No," Sasha said. "I've never even met him. Whatever you guys have gotten yourselves into, it must be bad."

CHAPTER
8

SASHA led them to a separate, smaller room to begin their training. "You're not ready for the Big Top yet."

"Big Top?" Ben asked.

"The large training room. We'll start you off in here first, and see what you can do."

Thick padding covered the walls, ceiling, and floor of the room. It had obviously seen many, many actuations. Burn marks, ragged holes, and water stains marred the padding as well as the cinder blocks peeking through.

"Let's start with some basics. What can you guys do? Peter?"

"With or without augmentation?"

"Without." Sasha put her hands on her hips. "Of course."

Ben looked at the floor. He knew what his answer would be when she asked him, and he dreaded it.

"Mostly Class One," Peter said. "I can move small objects. I've attempted some Class Two, but haven't had much success."

"Much?" Sasha raised an eyebrow. "Or any?"

"Any," Peter said.

"That's okay." Sasha bobbed her head. "Class One is where we all start. What about you, Ben?"

Ben scratched the edge of the bandage on his head. "Nothing."

"What do you mean?"

Ben frowned at his chest. "I can't actuate anything on my own."

Peter spoke up. "You should see him with augmentation, though. He can do Class Two actuations in his sleep. He shot a lightning bolt at one of the Dread Cloaks."

"Really?" Sasha touched her chin with one hand and cupped her elbow with the other. "Targeted lightning is pretty advanced, even with augmentation. You're sure you can't actuate without it?"

"I've tried," Ben said.

"That doesn't make sense to me. To do what you do . . ." She paused. "Maybe it's not the augmentation you need."

"What do you mean?" Ben asked.

"Maybe you just need a Locus."

"A what?"

"A Locus. A mental focal point to help you form the actuation. Some of the greatest Actuators in history have used them. Think of the classic image of a wizard."

"Hold on." Ben held up his hands. "You're not suggesting a wand, are you?"

Peter grinned. "Abracadabra."

"Don't be ridiculous," Sasha said. "You'd be laughed out of the League. A wand is completely impractical. But we may need to find you something that *will* work. Something small that you can tuck away in a pocket and hold on to if you need it."

"Okay." Ben still had doubts. "I guess it's worth a try."

"Good. I'll be right back. Wait here."

She left the room, while Peter and Ben remained, seated on the floor.

Peter rolled his gaze around the room. "Can you believe this? And that's not a rhetorical question. I mean, *can* you believe this?"

"Yes. But I don't think I really believed it until I saw my mom. She didn't know me. At all." The memory charged at him hard, but Ben held it back by reminding himself of the deal he had made with Agent Spear. "What they did to us was wrong."

"You saw the Dread Cloaks." Peter leaned close. "These are the good guys, Ben."

"Are they?"

"Yes. They are."

Ben scratched at his bandage. "This thing itches like crazy."

"Poole's the one that hit you." Peter sat back. "The League saved you."

"Hmm. Maybe."

"Maybe?"

Sasha came back into the room. "Here we go." She carried a small cardboard box that rattled as she sat down. "These are some things the League has collected and used in the past if someone needed a Locus. Look through it and see if anything grabs you."

Ben took the box in his lap and peered inside at an odd assortment of objects. There were toys, mostly metal soldiers, large marbles, crystals like the ones that hung from chandeliers, dice, magnets, balls, and other stuff. Ben rummaged through it.

"See anything you like?" Sasha asked.

"Nah." But then Ben spotted a curious rock. It was flat, polished smooth with rounded edges, in the shape of a long oval that fit nicely in the palm of his hand. In the middle it had a spiral fossil. Some kind of snail shell. Ben looked at it for a few moments and folded his fingers around it, gripping it in his fist. "This. I like this."

"Why that?"

Ben opened his fist and bounced the rock in his palm. "I like the weight. And the fossil shell kind of makes me think of actuation. Like a thought spiraling out from me."

"Sounds good." Sasha took the box and leaped to her feet. "Let's try it."

She took Ben to one side of the room, and positioned Peter behind them.

"Let's go for something simple," she said. "What were you particularly good at with the augmentation?"

"Rain," Peter said from behind them. "He made a rain cloud his first day."

Sasha looked at Ben.

He nodded.

"Rain it is," Sasha said. She gestured to the area in the middle of the room. "When you're ready."

Ben held out the Locus. "What am I supposed to do with this?"

"Imagine the stone is a lens, and your thoughts are rays of light passing through it. Or think of that fossil. Imagine your thoughts hitting the stone, and spiraling out from it."

Ben tightened his grip around the Locus, the rock warming up to match the temperature of his hand. He closed his eyes, and summoned the thoughts he always had to actuate rain. He saw the atoms, he combined them, he collected them, and a water vapor formed. He condensed it to where it formed a cloud. He opened his eyes.

Nothing. Nothing but a padded room and two people looking at him, expecting him to do something he didn't think he could do.

"Try again," Sasha said. "The Locus is an extension of you. It will work."

Ben's sigh was half growl. He closed his eyes again, and went through the same rain thoughts. But this time, he held the Locus out in front of him and imagined his thoughts passing through it. He squeezed his hand tightly around the stone. Tight enough he worried about how fragile it might be. Tight enough that his arm started to quiver after a few moments. But he kept his thoughts flowing, from his mind to the rock, through the spiral, radiating outward in waves.

"Open your eyes, Ben," Sasha said.

Ben opened them.

A small cloud churned in front of him. A cloud just like those he had made before.

"Nice," Peter said behind him.

Ben watched the cloud, and then looked at the Locus in his hand.

"Plenty of Actuators use them," Sasha said. "It's just a mental trick, really."

"A trick that worked," Ben said. *He had actuated.* It still felt like just another kind of augmentation, but that didn't matter. He could actuate now, *outside* Dr. Hughes's lab.

The rest of the training session went smoothly. He and Peter took turns demonstrating what they knew. Ben created snow, rain, fire; all the things he'd been able to do with Dr. Hughes's equipment, he could now do with his Locus. Peter performed his Class One actuations easily, but when he tried

Class Two actuations like Ben, he couldn't muster any to completion.

"Maybe it's just the way you learned how to do it," Sasha said. "Your mind is used to augmentation. Do you want to try a Locus, Peter? It might help you."

Peter scowled. "No."

"Are you sure?" Ben asked.

"I'm sure." Peter wiped his forehead with his sleeve. "I'll get it on my own."

Ben looked at the stone in his hand. "You're saying I'm not?"

Peter didn't answer.

"Not bad, boys," Sasha finally said at the end of the session. "Better than I was expecting. You'll be ready for the Big Top sooner than I thought. But not quite yet."

That evening, Sasha took Ben and Peter to the dining room. There were four round tables, each with four chairs, and far fewer agents and trainees than they had seen practicing in the Big Top that day. A few silver buffet servers sat on a table against one of the walls. Sasha led them to one end of the table, where they picked up plates, silverware, and napkins.

"Where is everybody?" Peter asked.

"Gone home." Sasha lifted the first hinged lid, releasing a cloud of steam. "Mmm. Pot roast. This is actually pretty good."

"Home?" Ben asked. His mom would be getting home about that time.

"Yeah. Some agents have families, some don't." Sasha dished up. "It's mostly only recruits and junior agents that live at headquarters." She lifted the lid of the next server. Mashed potatoes. "These are from a box, just so you know."

Ben helped himself to some of the pot roast. "But, what about being detached?"

"That's just when you're recruited," Sasha said. "After you're an agent, you have more options. You start a new life." The third server held the gravy. Sasha took the ladle and stirred in the skin that had formed over the top.

"Were you detached?" Ben asked. "When they recruited you?"

Sasha looked up at the wall, then let the silver lid fall with a loud clang. "Yup."

After the servers came a bowl of salad and some rolls. Sasha grabbed a handful of salad, literally, with her hand. She left Ben and Peter and went to one of the tables.

Peter tipped his head toward Ben, his voice a murmur. "I don't think she wants to talk about it."

"Yeah, I'm getting that," Ben said.

They both finished dishing up their plates and joined Sasha.

"Listen," Ben said. "I didn't mean to —"

"It's not a big deal." Her knee jackhammered under the table. "Really, don't worry about it. It's just the way it is. For all of us."

"Okay." But that didn't mean it was right. Ben reached for the salt.

"Personally," Peter said, "I've been wishing my parents would just forget about me for a while now. So this is perfect."

"Good for you, Class One," Sasha said.

Peter's mouth closed and his face flushed. Ben got mad. There wasn't any reason to embarrass or hurt Peter, even if he was going off when he shouldn't. Ben was about to speak up when Sasha closed her eyes and shook her head.

"I'm sorry. That wasn't right. I'm sorry." She tucked her hair behind her ears. "Let's just finish eating. Okay?"

"Okay," Ben and Peter said at once.

After dinner, they said good-bye to Sasha and joined the other male recruits and junior agents downstairs. The TV was on, and a couple of guys were trying to play pool in spite of the saggy table. Ben and Peter were introduced to everybody, watched some TV, and before long it was time for bed.

Ben lay awake for a while, hands folded behind his head. He couldn't sleep. He kept thinking about his mom. How she'd come home to an empty apartment, make who-knew-what for dinner, and after that she would have . . . Then it occurred to him. What she *wouldn't* be doing.

She would not be packing his lunch for the next day.

With that thought, Ben felt like something had jumped on his stomach. He kept himself from making any sounds, but he couldn't stop the tears or the pain. This was wrong. Peter was wrong about the League. They might be better than the Dread Cloaks in some ways.

But that didn't make them the good guys.

Morning started with breakfast in the same dining room, a solid mass of scrambled eggs in one server, a pile of very thin, almost translucent bacon in the other. There was juice, milk, and coffee, and a toaster you had to stand in line to use. Sasha sat with Ben and Peter, her sleek black hair pulled into a braid, the blue streak peeking in and out of it. She didn't say much, and Ben didn't know if it was because she was still upset, or if she just wasn't a morning person.

"What are we going to work on today?" Peter doused his eggs with Tabasco.

"More of the same." She sipped her coffee. "But it might be a good day to go over some basic history."

Peter stretched out the next few syllables. "Basic like Columbus sailing the ocean blue?"

"Not quite," Sasha said.

"There is something I've noticed, though," Peter said. "The League seems to do everything with paper. Where are all the computers?"

"The microprocessors in computers work because of quantum mechanics," Sasha said. "All the actuation going on around here fries them pretty quick, so they don't bother with them. Cell phones and TVs don't last long, either."

Agent Spear walked into the room a short while later, before they'd finished eating. He glanced around at everyone, and then said, "He's here."

Ben looked at Sasha.

"Mr. Weathersky," she said.

"He'd like to speak to everyone," Agent Spear said. "We're convening in the main training room in ten." Then he left.

Sasha looked at their plates. "Hurry and finish eating."

CHAPTER

9

BEN got down low and scooped heaps of egg into his mouth. Peter picked up a piece of bacon between two fingers and crunched. They each took a last swig of juice and followed Sasha from the dining room down the hallway to the Big Top. A portable podium now stood at one end of the room, while ranks of chairs covered the floor. Sasha led them up to one of the front rows. They took their seats and waited.

Within minutes, the room had filled. Ben started counting, trying to figure out how many agents and junior agents and recruits there were, but gave up. He guessed a couple hundred, at least.

The room filled with a thumping sound as Agent Spear tapped the microphone. "Please take your seats." He waited a moment. Ben sat up straighter in his chair. "Thank you all for coming. It is a rare honor to have a visit from the director of our agency. He certainly doesn't need any words of introduction from me, but I'd like to say a few, anyway. Like me, some of you can recall how it used to be. The League had fallen on hard times when Mr. Weathersky took up leadership. Corruption. Dwindling numbers. Poor recruiting methods. The gangs and crews and crime families were stronger than ever. But Mr. Weathersky pushed back the tide. He cleaned up the agency. He strengthened us and made us into what we are today, a League I am proud to belong to. Please join me in extending a very grateful welcome to Mr. Weathersky."

The room applauded, and Ben joined in as a man stepped up to the podium. He was tall and broad, like he might have just walked out of a comic book. Ben couldn't tell how old he was, but his white hair was peppered coal black, and deep wrinkles sprouted around his eyes. He wore a pale gray suit, and with the simple act of gripping the podium, he drew the attention of the whole room.

"Agents and recruits, ladies and gentlemen, I thank you for that welcome. I wanted to speak with you today to commend you for all the work you do. Agent Spear gave me far too much credit for what this agency has become." He nodded over the crowd. "It is not me but you, the soldiers on the front line, who have pushed back the tide. I am honored and humbled to league with you."

As he watched and listened to Mr. Weathersky, Ben knew what Peter had meant when he'd said you could sense an Actuator. Power emanated from the man at the podium. Sasha said he was one of the few who could actuate Class Threes, and Ben believed it.

Mr. Weathersky paused. "I wish I could say our job is done. But recent events, which I'm sure you've heard about, are all the evidence we need to know that crime and evil still exist, as dangerous as ever. There are still men and women who would use actuation for their own gain at the expense and pain of others."

He leaned forward over the podium, and Ben leaned backward from the force coming off him.

"But *we* are here." Mr. Weathersky stabbed the pulpit with a finger. "Stronger than ever. *We* stand against the evil in this world. *We* will hold them back with the wall of our Quantum League. Will you continue to stand with me?"

A collective shout of "Yes, sir!" erupted in patches around the room. Ben wanted to add his voice.

Mr. Weathersky smiled. He shouted, "Will you stand with me?"

"YES, SIR!" Ben cried, along with a room-wide chorus.

"Thank you for your service, ladies and gentlemen." Mr. Weathersky stepped away from the podium, and the room rose to its feet in applause.

Ben joined in. He couldn't help it. But then he realized

what he was doing. He started thinking that maybe he shouldn't be so enthusiastic about a man who had reformed the League's recruiting methods. What if detachment had been Mr. Weathersky's doing?

He looked over at Peter. His friend was clapping hard, smiling big, unaware of Ben or anyone else. It seemed he'd bought into this Weathersky guy completely. So had Sasha. By the looks of it, so had everyone else in that room. Ben looked back at the director, who now stood a few feet back, waving and nodding. Ben wondered if there was some kind of actuation that turned people into mindless sheep.

The applause eventually subsided, and the audience rose and began dispersing. Sasha turned to Ben and Peter.

"Ready, boys?"

"Hang on, there." Agent Spear walked over to them. "The director would like a few moments with them."

"He would?" Peter said.

"Why?" Ben asked.

"We have, intel on Dr. Hughes and the portable augmenter."

Ben jumped to his feet. "Where is she? Is she okay?"

"She's alive and unharmed, as far as we know," he said. "Come, we'll fill you in. And Mr. Weathersky has a few questions for you."

Ben looked at Peter. Peter looked at Sasha.

"Go," she said.

So they left the main training room and followed Agent Spear to the old church's former library. They found Mr. Weathersky already seated at a table, Agent Taggart next to him.

"Ah, Ben. Peter." Mr. Weathersky waved them over. "Come in, come in."

Agent Spear led them to the table, took the chair on the other side of the director, and motioned for Ben and Peter to sit across from them.

"I understand you two are our newest recruits?" Mr. Weathersky said.

"Yes, sir," Peter said. He kept his head bowed at an angle. So did Agent Taggart and Agent Spear. Did this man cast a spell over everyone?

"Well," Mr. Weathersky said. "I must take a moment to recognize and honor you. Detachment is not an easy thing. That policy direction was not taken lightly, I assure you. But the road to justice requires sacrifices from all of us, and it is likely that detachment is only the first of many you will be called upon to make to do what is right."

That sounded good. But it still felt all wrong.

Mr. Weathersky turned to Agent Taggart. "I understand these two are quite advanced for their age."

Agent Taggart smiled. "They are, sir."

"Excellent." He turned back to them. "How are you both settling in?"

Ben swallowed. Should he tell the truth?

But Peter spoke for both of them. "We're doing great, sir."

"Just wait." Mr. Weathersky leaned back in his chair, his hands before him, fingertips to fingertips. "As you deepen your understanding of the quantum realm, you press your ear to creation's door. The universe, as Sir James Jeans put it, will begin to look more like a great thought than a great machine."

The room went quiet after that.

Ben cleared his throat. "Agent Spear, you mentioned intel on Dr. Hughes?"

"Yes." He blinked. "Our sources have confirmed that the Dread Cloaks have taken her to one of their headquarters, along with the augmenter gun. Not only that, but there's some kind of rift between factions taking place within the gang."

"She's alive?" Mr. Weathersky asked.

"Yes." Agent Taggart spoke up. "Apparently, Poole believes the augmenter is not yet fully functional. He has kept her alive to make it so."

"I was told that it worked," Mr. Weathersky said.

"Ben assured us it was functional," Agent Taggart said.

Mr. Weathersky turned to him. "Is it?"

"I used it. It worked. It just didn't work the way Dr. Hughes thought it should."

Mr. Weathersky drummed his fingers on the table. "Tell me exactly what you did with it, and what happened."

Ben explained the range experiment that Dr. Hughes had set up, his actuating thoughts, and the ice missile they had produced. "Dr. Hughes stopped the tests at that point."

"I can see why," Mr. Weathersky said. "Now, tell me about the day of the attack on the lab."

So Ben, this time with Peter's input, told everything that had happened from the moment the Dread Cloaks entered the lab to when he and Peter lost consciousness.

"I'm impressed, Ben," Mr. Weathersky said. "You had the presence of mind in that situation to actuate a lightning bolt? Not many could have done that without much more extensive training."

"I had augmentation." Ben wasn't going to allow this man's flattery to get inside him.

"Even so," Mr. Weathersky said. "Is there anything else you can tell me? Anything about that day that stands out to you?"

Peter shrugged. "Dr. Hughes was late."

"Did she say why?" Mr. Weathersky asked.

"She said she'd been making contact with other researchers on the subject of portable augmentation."

That's right. Ben remembered that now. And there was one man, in particular. Someone she thought would be an ally. But what was his name?

"That must be how they found her," Agent Taggart said. "That's how she came to Poole's attention."

"Agreed," Mr. Weathersky said.

But Ben felt there had to be more to it than that. They were missing something, and it had to do with that other man. His name. *What was it?*

"What are your orders, sir?" Agent Spear asked.

"Before we proceed," Agent Taggart said, "should we dismiss Ben and Peter?"

"No." Mr. Weathersky stared at the table. "I believe they are an essential part of this operation. They both know Dr. Hughes. Ben knows the device, which is clearly too dangerous to remain in Dread Cloak hands."

Ben doubted Quantum League hands were any safer.

"A rescue mission?" Agent Taggart asked.

Mr. Weathersky shook his head. "Yes, but not a strike mission. Dr. Hughes will be too heavily guarded. This will have to be an inside job."

Agent Spear rubbed his chin. "We don't have any undercovers or assets in play that could get close enough."

"Is there anyone we could turn?" Mr. Weathersky asked. "Recruit a double agent."

"None of our current candidates are close enough to Poole," Agent Taggart said.

"Hold on now." Agent Spear sat forward. "We might have someone."

"Who is it?" Mr. Weathersky asked.

Agent Spear appeared to hesitate. "Ronin."

Agent Taggart snorted. "You must be joking."

Agent Spear said nothing.

She raised her voice. "Are you out of your mind?"

"If we had another three months for this operation," Agent Spear said, "we might be able to come up with someone else. But right now, I believe he's our only viable option."

Agent Taggart leaned an elbow on the table and pointed at Agent Spear. "You bring Ronin into this, and we might as well stage a full frontal assault. The operation will fail before it's even begun! What are you thinking, Greg?"

"Have you got any better ideas?"

Mr. Weathersky held up his hands like Ben's teachers did to break up a fight.

The agents fell silent.

"It will only be a matter of time," Mr. Weathersky said, "before the gun is augmenting with accuracy and efficiency. We must move quickly, and consider all options. Agent Spear, will you bring me the dossier on Ronin?"

Agent Spear rose from his chair. "Yes, sir." He left the room.

After he'd left, Agent Taggart put her hand on the table. "Sir, I —"

"Class Three actuations, Agent Taggart." Mr. Weathersky looked hard at her. Ben sensed a change in the waves coming off him. He wasn't commanding loyalty right now. He was commanding respect and fear. How did he do that?

The director continued. "If Poole gets that gun working, the Dread Cloaks will be operating with Class Three actuations. We're talking about terrible storms. Tornadoes. Maybe even small earthquakes. What will we do then?"

Earthquakes. Something tickled Ben's mind. That man. His name.

"I do understand that, sir," Agent Taggart said. "But I also know Ronin."

What was the name?

Agent Spear returned a moment later with a thick file in his hand. He handed it to Mr. Weathersky and took his seat. "Ethan Morrow, aka Ronin. Former Quantum Agent, went rogue nearly fifteen years ago. Since then, he's operated on several heist crews working low-level crime. Staying under the radar."

Mr. Weathersky flipped through the file. "Where is he now?"

"Last known affiliation was the Paracelsus crew," Agent Spear said. "As far as we know, he's still heading them up. An anonymous tip came in a week ago. Ronin's planning a jewel heist soon. Intel says it's legit."

"All right," Mr. Weathersky said. "What makes you think he could get close to Poole and Dr. Hughes?"

"He and Poole ran on a crew together ten years ago when Poole was just starting out in the Dread Cloaks."

Mr. Weathersky looked up at the ceiling. "The old True Coat crew, if I'm not mistaken."

"That's correct, sir," Agent Spear said. "We caught them in a heist and nabbed Ronin. Everyone else escaped. Ronin eventually escaped, too, but the point is, he could have rolled on the rest of the crew when he was in custody and he didn't."

"So you think Poole will trust him," Mr. Weathersky said.

"As far as Poole trusts anyone," Agent Spear said.

Mr. Weathersky closed the file. "And you think we could turn Ronin?"

"With the proper leverage, yes."

Agent Taggart laughed. "You'll never turn him. He *can't* be turned. He's in it for himself."

Mr. Weathersky closed his eyes and squeezed the bridge of his nose with two fingers. "Break the operation down for me. Likelihood of success, scale of one to ten. Agent Taggart?"

Scale. The tickling in Ben's mind returned.

"If Ronin is involved," she said, "it's a nonstarter. Zero."

Scale. Earthquake.

Mr. Weathersky turned to Agent Spear. "Same question."

"Realistically," he said, "four or five, sir. But it's still the only option available."

The name was right there. Ben could almost grab it. It was . . .

"I agree. Until we come up with another solution, we'll move forward with —"

"Richter!" Ben said.

Everyone turned to look at him.

"Sorry." Ben bowed his head. "I've been trying to remember that name."

The two agents looked at each other. They looked at Mr. Weathersky. Mr. Weathersky looked right into Ben's eyes.

"And why would you be trying to remember *that* name?"

Ben felt the director's gaze like a hot wind in his face. "I, uh — I mean, that was the guy. The guy who was going to help Dr. Hughes with portable augmentation."

He looked to Peter for agreement, but Peter just looked confused.

Agent Spear chewed on a corner of his lip. "You don't suppose . . ."

"Don't be ridiculous," Agent Taggart said. "Poole probably used the name to cover his tracks. Richter doesn't exist."

"What do you mean?" Ben asked.

"Richter," Mr. Weathersky said, "is supposedly a powerful criminal overlord. A mastermind. When we first heard of him, we tried to find out who he was. We dedicated an entire unit of agents to that purpose, and after years of work, they had nothing to show for it. We concluded that Richter is a kind of gangster tall tale, a bogeyman, and we closed the case."

"And yet," Agent Spear said, "the finest trick of the devil is to persuade you that he does not exist."

"Baudelaire?" Mr. Weathersky said. "I'm impressed, Agent Spear. Nevertheless, let us concentrate on the devil we do know."

Agent Spear nodded. "Poole."

"Ronin," Agent Taggart said.

Mr. Weathersky frowned. "Make that two devils."

CHAPTER 10

"YOU really don't remember?" Ben and Peter stood outside their smaller training room, waiting for Sasha. "Richter?"

"The name doesn't sound familiar at all," Peter said. "I wasn't going to contradict you in there, but I didn't know what you were talking about."

"But you were there."

Peter's smile was crooked and apologetic. "Sorry."

Ben gave up, frustrated. He was certain the name was important, somehow. He couldn't say how, he just felt it. He didn't want to forget it again, so every few minutes, he repeated it a few times in his head.

Richter.

Richter.

Richter.

After a few times of this, the name stopped feeling so slippery. Like a noodle drying, it stuck to the wall of his brain.

"Change of plans, boys." Sasha marched toward them down the hallway. "No history lesson today. You're to be field-ready ASAP. Mr. Weathersky's orders."

"Why?" Ben asked.

"Weren't you in that meeting? They just briefed me, and the three of us will be part of the operation to take down the Paracelsus crew."

Ben had said it before, but he guessed he needed to say it again. "Sasha, I'm twelve."

Peter opened his mouth, probably to say he would be thirteen next month, but Sasha cut him off.

"You won't be engaging directly. The director just wants you present, and I'm supposed to babysit you."

Ben hadn't had a babysitter in years. He certainly didn't need one now. But his resentment wasn't as strong as his curiosity. "If we're not engaging, then why are we going?"

Sasha opened the training room door. "Mr. Weathersky thinks you're important to this operation."

"How?" Peter asked as the three of them entered.

"It all comes down to entanglement," she said. "You and Dr. Hughes. You and Poole. You and the portable augmenter. You're involved. And you can't play the game if you don't have all the pieces on the board."

So they were all just pieces to Mr. Weathersky? Ben fought the urge to walk out of there, right then. But thoughts of his mom kept him in that room. He would do whatever it took for the League to give him back his life. He also thought of Dr. Hughes. If he could do something to help her, he would do it.

"Let's get started," he said.

Over the next several days, when they weren't in their beds or the dining room, Ben and Peter were with Sasha in their training room. With his Locus in his hand, Ben continued to refine his actuations. The more he practiced, the more automatic they became, and the faster he got.

He learned to not only form a fireball, but to shoot it forward at a target. He learned to actuate rain to extinguish the fireballs Sasha shot at him. He learned how to fight using actuations, the way the agents fought with the Dread Cloaks and the heist crews.

Peter had a harder time of it. He continued to refuse a Locus, but was eventually able to actuate some Class Twos without one. Nothing nearly as big and powerful as Ben's, and he was really slow at it, but it was something.

"You're getting it," Ben said at the end of a grueling day. They were on the stairs heading down to the barracks, and all he could think about was his bed.

"Thanks," Peter said. But his voice was edged with something. Anger? Sarcasm?

Ben stopped on the stairwell. "What's wrong?"

"Nothing."

"Tell me."

Peter didn't look at him. "I've just never been the slow one, all right?"

"I knew it was bothering you."

"Of course it's bothering me."

"Well, don't let it. It doesn't matter how fast or how slow you are. All that matters is —"

Peter held up a hand like a crossing guard. "Deep down, everybody wants to be the hare. Who *wants* to be the tortoise? I don't care what the fable says." He moved on down the stairs.

Ben sighed and followed after him. They didn't talk for the rest of the night, but Ben was kept awake, trying to figure out how he could help Peter feel better. His dad had really messed with his head. He believed he wasn't worth anything if he wasn't the smartest, the fastest, the best.

Thinking about it made Ben sad, and he fell asleep worrying about his friend.

It seemed Ben had barely closed his eyes when someone was shaking him awake, shining a flashlight in his face. He blinked and shielded his eyes with his hands. What were the other guys doing?

"Get that out of my face," he said.

"Up and at 'em, son." Agent Spear's voice.

Ben sat up. The man stood over him dressed in the same military gear Ben had seen the League wearing in Dr. Hughes's lab.

"That's right," Agent Spear said. "Tonight's the night."

Ben threw off his covers and jumped out of bed. In the slanted light from the flashlight, shadows deepened Peter's grin into something a little wild. They both hustled into their clothes; Ben made sure he had his Locus, and they followed Agent Spear upstairs. He took them to a part of the building they'd never been to before.

"Time to get you boys suited up."

He unlocked a door and let them into a room filled with the kind of gear the agent was wearing. There was a long bench in the middle of the room, with two suits laid out.

"These are the smallest size we have," he said. "Hopefully, they won't be too big on you."

Ben and Peter examined the uniforms. They were made of a thick black canvas, with plates and pads of armor sewn in. They were heavy, and took some getting used to once Agent Spear had helped Ben and Peter get dressed. Ben looked down at himself, and bent his arms and his legs to test his range of motion. The suit actually fit him pretty well.

"They're insulated against electricity and cold," the agent said. "And they're fire resistant. The armor will stop most projectiles."

Projectiles?

Ben tried not to show the fear that began seeping in through the pads and protection of the suit.

"Uh-oh," Peter said. "I should have peed before I put this on, shouldn't I?"

"That's a good habit to get into." Agent Spear grinned. "Now, take these."

He handed them each a helmet like the ones policemen used during riots, the kind with a clear plastic shield in front. They tried them on. Ben's was a bit big, but if he cinched up the strap it stayed in place.

"Ready?" Agent Spear asked.

"I was serious." Peter took off his helmet. "I have to go."

"Do you need help with the suit?" Ben could hear the smirk in the agent's voice.

"I think I can manage," Peter said.

"Go. Meet us in the main training room."

Peter left, and Ben went with Agent Spear. When they entered the Big Top, they found several others already there, all dressed for combat. Ben saw Agent Taggart, and half a dozen other agents, most of whom he didn't recognize.

Sasha came up beside him. "Where's Class One?"

"Don't call him that," Ben said. It came out sharper than he meant it to.

"Sorry. I didn't think he'd mind, now that he's moved on to Class Two. Sometimes a little teasing gets you fired up. Works for me."

"Yeah, well. Not for him. Just leave it alone, okay?"

"Fine. Okay."

A charged silence followed.

"You ready for this?" Sasha asked.

"You're my trainer. You tell me."

"Hmm. I don't know." She stood back and looked at him with her head cocked at an exaggerated angle, her hand on her chin. "Is that a woman's uniform?"

"WHAT?"

"Kidding. Relax, Locus Boy. You're more than ready for what we're going to be doing."

Ben took a deep breath. "How many of these have you been on?"

"Me? This is my first."

"Really?"

Sasha's nod was a bit more tense than usual. "I've gone on lots of patrols. But this is my first full operation."

Ben realized that maybe Sasha's teasing was actually to relieve her own stress. He could tell she was trying to look confident, but maybe she didn't feel that way on the inside.

She shifted on her feet. "But I was up for my Trials in a couple of months, anyway."

"Trials?"

"Before they promote you from junior agent to full agent, you have to go on three operations. They have to see how you perform in the field. Agent Taggart said this will count as my first."

"I'm sure you'll do fine," Ben said.

"You better hope so." She winked at him. "My job is to protect you two."

Ben saw Peter come into the room and waved him over.

"Don't tell Agent Spear," he said as he approached them, "but I did need help with the suit."

Sasha made a show of looking him over. "Aside from having it on backward, you look great."

Peter looked at her, and then at Ben. "She's kidding, right?"

"Get used to it," Ben said.

"Listen up, people!" Agent Spear stood with his arms folded across his chest. Everyone in the room turned to face him. "You've all been briefed, but remember: Ronin is the target, and the mission is acquisition. The other members of the crew are secondary. The jewels are secondary. If it means catching Ronin, you let the jewels and the other members of his crew go free."

Agent Taggart stepped up beside him. "Ronin is a former agent. Consider him extremely dangerous. He knows our tactics, and he'll use that against you. Use extreme caution, keep radio contact, and *don't* try to take him on your own. Understood?"

The agents nodded around the room.

Ben felt a quivering in his chest. He reached into his pocket and rolled the Locus stone into his fist.

"The vans are waiting," Agent Spear said. "Let's move out."

The agents formed into a loose column and headed out the door. Sasha turned to Ben and Peter. "Ready, boys?"

"Ready," Peter said.

"Ready," Ben said.

She led them after the agents to the rear of the building, where three black vans idled in the night. Agents piled into them.

"Agent Lambert." Agent Spear waved them over to his vehicle. "You guys are with me."

They climbed into the van, and Sasha, Ben, and Peter took up one of the benches. It was tight. Sasha sat between them, staring straight ahead, and Ben could feel her knee bouncing against his. From the first time he'd seen her practicing in the Big Top, she'd seemed much older than him. As their trainer, she seemed so much more experienced. But right now, she didn't seem very different.

"How old are you?" Ben asked her.

"What?"

"How old are you?"

"Sixteen." She frowned. "Why?"

"Just curious."

"Look, I've been in the League since I was your age. I can handle this."

Ben shook his head. "That's not what I meant. I —"

"That's everyone." Agent Spear climbed into the front passenger seat. He turned to the driver. "Let's go."

• • •

It was late enough, or early enough, depending on how you counted it, that the city streets were pretty deserted. The few buses they passed still running at that hour were almost empty. The vans glided by darkened storefronts, apartments, and other buildings. At another time, Ben might have liked the feeling of being out while the world around him slept. But tonight, every shadow and every black window held something sinister within.

No one spoke. With each mile, the tension inside the van mounted. Like when his mom used that cooker to can blueberries from the farm. Ben felt the silence like a pressure on his ears.

A short while later, Agent Spear leaned forward. "We're here. Slow down, and pull into that alley." He pointed the way.

The driver killed the headlights and eased the van into a black rift. The other vans followed in a column behind them.

After they'd come to a stop, Spear looked back at Sasha, Ben, and Peter. "You remember your orders, Agent Lambert?"

"Yes, sir."

Agent Spear nodded, opened his door, and slipped out of the vehicle. The agents sitting behind them opened the van's sliding door and climbed out after him. Ben turned around and watched them form up and stalk from the alley.

A handheld radio hissed to life in Sasha's hand. She adjusted the volume, and the sounds of footsteps, movement, and hushed voices came through.

"What are your orders?" Ben whispered.

"Sit tight," Sasha said. "Keep you safe. Only intervene if given no other options."

"Then why are we here, again?" Peter asked.

"Pieces in a game," Ben said.

They sat listening to the radio for a while. Not much seemed to be happening out there.

And then they heard Agent Taggart's voice come through. "Approaching the building now."

"The jewels are in a bank around the corner," Sasha whispered. "Scheduled for transfer tomorrow. Right now, the agents will be trying to gain access without being spotted by Ronin's lookout."

The radio squealed and clanged with the sound of metal. Then silence.

"We're in." That was Agent Spear's voice. "All agents with me."

Ben's heartbeat quickened. He leaned closer to the radio. So did Peter.

Silence followed. The agents were inside the bank now, closing in on the Paracelsus crew. Ben imagined them advancing forward with hand signals.

Peter took a breath. "What —?"

"Shh!" Sasha said.

The radio went quiet, so quiet Ben thought it might have switched off. It stayed that way for a long time. But then an explosion of sound ripped through it, a roar of static and shouts.

Ben jumped.

"What's going on?" Peter asked.

Sasha gripped the radio. "They've engaged the crew in combat."

"Target on the move!" Agent Spear shouted. "All agents pursue!"

Sasha looked over her shoulder down the alley. She bit her lip. "Put on your helmets."

Ben and Peter did as she ordered.

They listened to more sounds of fighting. Actuations exploding through the radio speaker, one after the other, then simultaneously.

"Agent down!" That was Agent Taggart. "McNeil is down!"

Sasha covered her mouth.

"Agent Lambert!" That was Agent Spear. "Sasha, listen to me! The target is coming your way."

CHAPTER
11

SASHA tossed the radio aside and grabbed her helmet. "Stay in the van," she said. "And keep hidden." She climbed over Peter, pushed the door open, and slipped out into the alley. She looked terrified.

Ben moved to follow her. "We'll come with you."

"No!" she hissed. She peered toward the street. "Stay here."

"We should do what she says." Peter looked even more scared than she did.

Sasha took a deep breath and crept down the alley. Ben punched the seat. He felt helpless, like he had back in Dr. Hughes's lab when the Dread Cloaks attacked. He wanted to do something.

Sasha took up a defensive position against the grille of the van behind them. Ben guessed she was loading an actuation. Which was what he should be doing.

Agent Taggart squawked through the radio. "Agent Lambert! We took out the crew's getaway. The target is coming for a van. You need to get out of there, now!"

Ben looked at Peter. Peter just shook his head.

The silhouettes of two men appeared at the alley's entrance. One of them had to be Ronin, but which one? Ben looked at Sasha. She was peering around the edge of the vehicle, her hands balled up into fists. She was getting ready to attack. Where were the other agents? Where were Taggart and Spear?

"I told you," one of the silhouettes said. "Still the same playbook. Not even guarded."

Sasha leaped out and fired off a lightning bolt. It arced down the alley, lighting it up in a flash. But it missed and struck the brick wall. The two silhouettes dove for cover between the other vans.

Sasha pulled back to her position.

"We've got to help her," Ben said.

Peter shook his head. "I'm not good enough."

A fireball blazed past the van's door, striking a dumpster farther down the alley. They could escape that way. Ronin only wanted a vehicle.

Sasha shot off another lightning bolt. The two men returned fire. It went on like that for a few rounds. And then the van Sasha hid behind lurched. It started rolling forward. One of the men had actuated it into gear. Sasha moved with it a few steps, but if she didn't get out of the way, it was going to pin her against Ben and Peter's van.

She dove free just before the van hit, jolting Ben. Their attackers were waiting. A fireball struck Sasha in the chest and sent her flying backward.

"NO!" Ben shouted. "We've got to help her."

"Look." Peter pointed, and through the vans' windows Ben saw the two silhouettes climb into the last van. "They're leaving."

"They're getting away!" Ben said.

He jumped out into the alley, pulled out his Locus, and readied a lightning bolt of his own. He grabbed a swarm of electrons around him, balled them up, and slipped down toward the two men.

Their van's engine roared.

Ben had to act now. He leaped into view and fired the lightning bolt straight at the van's grille. It struck its target, and the engine choked and died smoking. He'd done it. He'd stopped them.

But now what?

The two men burst from the van. Ben could feel their actuations forming, that same change in the air he'd sensed from Poole. Ben was about to form another actuation of his own when a little fireball sputtered over his head toward the two men, where it smoked out harmlessly on the ground between them.

"I told you I wasn't good enough," Peter said from behind him.

"Fall back." Ben actuated another lightning bolt, but it missed.

One of the men shot a fireball of his own, but Ben was able to actuate a shield of water. It stopped the fireball in a flash of steam, but most of the water splashed to the ground in a puddle at his feet.

Ben looked down and felt what was about to happen, but he couldn't do anything to stop it. In that instant, one of the men shot a lightning bolt. The bolt arced and struck the puddle beneath him. Ben flinched.

Nothing happened. The suit had protected him. But that maneuver — fire, countered with water, then electricity — had been planned. He and Peter were clearly outmatched.

"Morrow!" Agent Spear's voice echoed toward them.

The two men looked behind them, then charged forward into the alley. One of them flew by before Ben could react, but Ben jumped in front of the other one. They collided, and both went down hard. The impact had forced the air from Ben's lungs. He gasped as the man got to his feet first. Ben felt him actuating as he came into view for the first time, but Ben was too dazed to do anything. He braced himself, hoping Peter had gotten clear.

But there was no actuation.

"You're just a kid," the man said.

Ben looked up. The man had close-cropped hair and a face that looked like someone had left it outside for too long. Ben felt the actuation fading as the man shook his head.

"So this is what they've come to," he said.

"Hold it right there, Morrow!" Agent Taggart shouted.

She, Spear, and three other agents entered the alley.

The man smiled at Ben. He put up his hands. "It's Ronin, if you don't mind. I haven't been Morrow for a long, long time."

"Call it in." Agent Spear was panting. "Tell Mr. Weathersky the target is acquired. We got him."

"Sasha!" Ben took off deeper into the alley, but before he'd gone more than a few steps, he saw her walking toward him, one arm around Peter's shoulders. "You're okay?" he asked her.

She nodded. "I might not have any eyebrows, but the suit did its job."

Police sirens howled in the distance.

"Ennays," Agent Spear said. "Let's clear out."

They all loaded into the two working vans. Five agents rode with Ronin in one of them, while Ben, Peter, and Sasha rode with Agents Spear, Taggart, and McNeil. McNeil had taken a lightning bolt that had fried his suit and knocked him out for a bit, but he was alive and relatively unharmed.

"Well done, all of you," Agent Spear said after they'd

gotten on the road. "Agent Lambert, consider your first Trial passed. With a commendation."

Sasha sighed. "Thank you, sir."

"I think what she did should count for two Trials," Peter said. "At least."

Agent Taggart chuckled, and it was the first time Ben had heard the woman laugh. "Perhaps you're right."

Agent Spear turned to Ben. "What you did was remarkable, son. You stood your ground against two hardened criminals. One of them a former Quantum Agent."

"Peter was right beside me," Ben said.

"Then that goes for Peter, too," Agent Spear said.

But the truth was that neither Ben nor Peter had decided the outcome that night. Ronin had stopped. He was about to finish Ben, could have done so easily, but he stopped himself. Because Ben was just a kid.

"What's to stop Ronin from actuating right now?" Peter asked. "What if he tries to escape?"

"I'd like to see him try," Agent Taggart said. "Each of the five agents in that van has an actuation ready to let loose on him if he moves a muscle."

But in sparing Ben, Ronin had basically turned himself in. "Agent Spear." Ben leaned forward. "I don't think Ronin —"

"Let it settle, son," Agent Spear said. "When we get back to headquarters, Mr. Weathersky will want a full report. For now, just let it settle. We'll get Ronin into a cell, and then we can all breathe easy."

"A cell?" Peter asked.

"A prison cell," Agent Taggart said. "A room that neutralizes actuating thoughts. The opposite of augmentation."

Ben sat back. He was confused, unsure of what to think about Ronin now. Maybe it was best to do like Agent Spear suggested, and let it settle.

They met Mr. Weathersky in the library. He debriefed the other agents first about what had gone down in the bank.

Apparently, the raid had been smooth, right up until the moment the agents were set to ambush Ronin and his men. That was when they realized Ronin had brought an additional member onto the Paracelsus crew, a man the League hadn't known about. Which meant there was an extra lookout.

The agents had lost the advantage of surprise, and that was all the edge Ronin had needed to make an escape.

"We immobilized his transport," Agent Taggart said. "So Ronin went looking for ours. Agent Spear radioed a warning to Agent Lambert."

Mr. Weathersky turned to Sasha. "Who I understand has just passed her first Trial, correct?"

"Yes, sir," Sasha said.

"Very good." He addressed the room. "I'd like to talk with Agent Lambert, Ben, and Peter now. Agents Spear and

Taggart, you will remain here as well. The rest of you are dismissed." The other agents filed from the room. "And get some rest, Agent McNeil."

After they'd gone, Mr. Weathersky stood. "Agent Spear tells me you all performed admirably. Vastly exceeding our expectations of ones so young."

So young. The very thing that had stalled Ronin.

Mr. Weathersky turned to Sasha. "Tell me what happened after you received the radio warning, Agent Lambert."

Sasha recounted her fight with Ronin and the other man. She told it how Ben remembered seeing it, in detail and objectively. Her report stopped when she got hit by the fireball and thrown backward.

"At which time" — Mr. Weathersky turned to Ben — "you engaged the target?"

"Yes," Ben said. "I didn't want to let him escape. I . . . immobilized their transport. I mean, the League's transport. The van they were trying to steal."

"And then what?"

Ben described the subsequent actuations, and how Ronin and his partner had gotten the upper hand. How they had tried to escape on foot when they'd heard Agent Spear. And how Ben had tripped him up. "He was about to kill me," Ben said. "I think he would have, but he stopped when he saw how young I was."

"Is that so?" Mr. Weathersky asked.

Ben nodded. "He said it."

"Perhaps," Mr. Weathersky said, "Ethan Morrow still has a conscience of some kind."

"Not likely," Agent Taggart said. "He was probably just caught off guard that a kid had been holding his own against him."

Ben wouldn't say he'd been holding his own. The whole thing could have easily gone a different way.

"Even so, we may be able to use that." Mr. Weathersky turned to Agent Spear. "It's time to initiate the next phase of this operation. I'd like to speak with Mr. Morrow. And I'd like for Ben to accompany me."

"Sir?" Agent Taggart said.

"Me?" Ben asked. Why would Mr. Weathersky want him?

Mr. Weathersky adjusted the lapels of his pale gray suit. "Ben threw Morrow off balance once. Perhaps he will again."

It seemed Ben was still just a piece on the board.

Mr. Weathersky crossed to the door. "Come, Ben."

Agent Spear nodded for him to go. Ben looked at Sasha and Peter. They both just stared. Perhaps they were still settling. Ben wished he could settle. He wanted nothing more now than to go downstairs and collapse on his bed.

But he followed Mr. Weathersky instead. "Coming, sir."

They went down the hallway to a door Ben hadn't ever used. It had its own lock, and Mr. Weathersky inserted a simple key. Ben guessed the actuations in the building fried the circuits in electronic locks like they did computers. The door opened onto metal stairs leading downward, most likely to a different part of the basement than their sleeping quarters.

Their footsteps echoed up and down the stairwell as they descended. When they reached the bottom, Mr. Weathersky unlocked another door, and they entered a white hallway. Three agents in combat suits stood guard down its length. They snapped to attention when they saw Mr. Weathersky.

"As you were, gentlemen." Mr. Weathersky went to the first door. He turned to Ben. "He can't harm you here. There's no need to worry."

"I wasn't," Ben said.

"Good." Mr. Weathersky opened the door, and Ben followed him inside.

CHAPTER
12

THE cell was about the size of their small training room. Ronin stood in the center, inside a clear box of a cage. He had a cot and a toilet in there with him, but not much else. He was in his socks, his boots tucked under the bed. As they got closer, Ben saw thin golden wires embedded in the plastic walls of his prison. Perhaps those had something to do with how the cell neutralized actuation.

Ronin raised an eyebrow at Mr. Weathersky. "The Old One comes to see me? This is an unexpected honor. What brings you down from on high? Something big must be happening."

"Hello, Ethan," Mr. Weathersky said.

Ronin looked around. "This cell is an upgrade from when I was last here."

"Your previous escape showed us our design's weak-nesses."

Ronin looked at Ben. "I see you're starting them even younger now. Who's the prodigy?"

Prodigy?

"This is Ben," Mr. Weathersky said. "Our newest recruit."

"I'm surprised you're not just stealing them from hospi-tal cribs by now."

"Don't be vulgar, Ethan," Mr. Weathersky said.

"It's Ronin, now." He sat down on his cot. "And how are your grandchildren doing in the League?"

"You can change your name, Ethan, but that doesn't change who you are. And to answer the implication that I am unwilling to make the same sacrifices I ask of others, let me say that I have lost many friends and loved ones in the line of duty." He paused. "As have you."

Ronin looked up. His face bore an instant look of such hatred and anger it made Ben take a step backward. Mr. Weathersky didn't move.

"Don't you dare." Ronin's whisper sounded like a wind that threatened to storm. "You of all people. Don't you dare."

"I don't mean to hurt you," Mr. Weathersky said. "I only meant to say that I know something of what you went through fifteen years ago, when you lost —"

Ronin flew at them and slammed the wall with his fists. "DON'T YOU DARE SAY THEIR NAMES!"

"— your wife and daughter." Mr. Weathersky never even flinched.

Tears formed in Ronin's eyes. His fists squeaked down the plastic wall. Ben wondered what had happened to his family fifteen years ago. That was the same time he had gone rogue. The two events had to be related.

Mr. Weathersky cleared his throat. "I can see your pain is as fresh today as it was then. Perhaps you're still trying to run from it."

"Why have you brought me here?" Ronin asked. "To torture me?"

"I told you, I don't mean to hurt you. In fact, I've come because I may be able to bring you some comfort."

"You?" Ronin laughed. "You really don't get it."

"I know you blame me." Mr. Weathersky took a step toward the cage. "But your daughter is alive, Ethan."

"What?"

"Eva is alive."

"Stop." Ronin held up his hands. "Just shut your mouth. I don't know what this is. Some kind of twisted revenge against the agent who turned against you? Well, it's not going to work on me."

"She's alive, Ethan."

"I saw their bodies." Fresh tears came, and Ben could tell Ronin was seeing the bodies now. "I saw what they —" Ronin clamped his mouth shut.

"There were two bodies, yes." Mr. Weathersky's voice sounded gentle. "One, I am heartbroken to say, was your wife. But the other was not your daughter. In the condition you found . . . They wanted you to think it was your daughter so you wouldn't come after them."

"No." Ronin had gone pale. He shook his head without taking his eyes off Mr. Weathersky. "No, you're lying."

"I am not lying."

"You're lying!" Ronin punched the wall again.

"I am not lying, Ethan. We found her a few months later, alive, when we raided the Abandon crew's safe house."

"If that were true, why did you wait until now to tell me?"

"By the time we found her, you had already gone rogue. You were *unfit*. She became a ward of the League."

Ronin leaned his forehead against the wall, closed his eyes, and rolled his head back and forth. "Why are you doing this?"

Ben pitied him, and he had to wonder the same thing. In the space of a few minutes, Mr. Weathersky had emotionally ripped this man open. Was that another ability the director had?

"Because I need something from you, Ethan," Mr. Weathersky said. "And I need it badly enough I'm willing to give you something in return. That is another reason why I have waited until now to tell you about your daughter."

Ronin pulled away from the wall. "Show her to me."

"I'm afraid that wouldn't be —"

"Bring her here, Old One!" Ronin spread his arms. "If she's alive, why can't I see her?"

Mr. Weathersky's lips tightened.

"That's what I thought," Ronin said. Ben could almost see him rebuilding his defenses. Driving back the pain.

"If I bring her here," Mr. Weathersky said, "will you help us?"

"If you bring my daughter here, I'll do anything you want." Ronin grinned, and his face wrinkled the way the leather of an old boot bent. "I'll put on a costume and be the Quantum League's mascot."

"Very well," Mr. Weathersky said. "Come, Ben."

They turned to leave.

"Boy, something has you spooked," Ronin said. "The Weathersky I remember would never have made a deal with a rogue agent, and he certainly never would've let one set the terms." Ronin looked at Ben. "Does it have something to do with him? Why did you bring him here?"

Mr. Weathersky returned to face Ronin. "You are right. Something does have me . . . spooked. The Dread Cloaks have kidnapped a professor. Ben's teacher."

"What else?" Ronin asked.

"She's not an Actuator. She's an innocent quantum physicist."

"And?"

"And," Mr. Weathersky said, "she may have developed the technology for portable augmentation."

"And there it is," Ronin said. He brought his hands together and started cracking his knuckles one at a time. "I see it now. Yeah, this is big. Big enough for you to get involved, that's for sure. And you want me to infiltrate the Dread Cloaks, right? Be your inside man with Poole?"

Ben was amazed. Ronin had figured out their entire strategy in a matter of moments.

"Yes," Mr. Weathersky said.

"What's your timeline?" Ronin asked.

"Imminent threat," Mr. Weathersky said. "We need immediate insertion. Which is why we came after your crew."

Ronin leaned in close to the wall. "How *did* you know about the job tonight?"

"An anonymous tip came in last week. Someone on your crew must have loose lips."

"No one on my crew. We've been together too long. If they were going to rat me out, they would have done it a long time ago."

"My agents said you had an extra man tonight."

"Extra man?" Ronin frowned. Then his eyes opened wide. "Oh, right. That guy. Inside man at the bank. The job was his idea. It was supposed to be clean, in and out."

"You're getting sloppy, Ethan," Mr. Weathersky said. "Letting strangers on your crew."

"He wasn't a stranger, he was . . ." Ronin scratched his head. "He was one of yours, wasn't he? You set me up."

Mr. Weathersky shook his head. "But it seems that someone did."

Ronin let out a one-breath laugh. Then he put his hands in his pockets. "Okay. I'll do it."

"Do what?" Mr. Weathersky asked.

"I'll be your inside man with Poole," Ronin said. "And when the job is done, you give me my daughter."

"So you believe me?" Mr. Weathersky asked.

Ronin swallowed, and a shade of his earlier grief returned. "Even you wouldn't lie about something like that."

Ben wanted to believe that, too. That there was a limit to what the Quantum League would do.

Ronin grabbed his boots from under the cot, sat down, and pulled one of them on. "I'll need someone in there with me."

"Of course," Mr. Weathersky said. "We'll find an agent to —"

"No. No agents." Ronin pulled on his other boot. "I want him." He nodded toward Ben.

"Me?" Ben shook his head, confused. What could Ronin want with him?

"Yes, you." Ronin stood, an inch or two taller with his boots. "I'm going to bring the Dread Cloaks a recruit, and you will look and play the part."

"But Poole knows me," Ben said. "I shot a lightning bolt at one of his men."

"That's even better," Ronin said.

"Better?" Ben wanted to help Dr. Hughes, but Ronin's plan sounded like suicide. "How is that better?"

"You're going to pretend to be a League defector." Ronin began recracking his knuckles.

"They'll suspect he's an undercover," Mr. Weathersky said. "You, too."

"Of course they will," Ronin said. "And we'll get caught. But then Ben will convince them that he *really* wants to defect, and he'll become a triple agent. Poole's been trying to get someone on the inside of the League for a while now. He will want to believe Ben is his man, and it's easy to get someone to believe something they want to believe."

Ben didn't like where this was going. It wasn't that he didn't trust Ronin. The man could have hurt him or even killed him in that alley. But Ben remembered Poole's blue eyes searing him through the ski mask, and he was scared. Scared to leave Peter and Sasha, scared of the Dread Cloaks, scared of Poole.

"What do you think, Ben?" Mr. Weathersky asked.

If it was Ben's decision, he had his answer. "Mr. Weathersky, I don't think I can."

"Then you better suit up," Ronin said. "Call in every agent you have for a battle, Old One, and expect it to get ugly. My plan is the only inside job that'll work."

"You're right, Ethan." Mr. Weathersky sighed. He took Ben by the shoulders, towering over him, and Ben felt that same power emanating from him. "A direct assault would result in many casualties. Do you understand? Brave men and women, like Agent Spear and Agent Taggart. Like your trainer, Sasha. I don't think you want that. I believe in you, Ben."

Ben knew what the man was doing. He could feel it, and it wasn't going to work. Ben was still just a piece in his game. Mr. Weathersky had brought Ben down here to keep him on the board, and had now found a way to play him. Well, Ben wasn't going to be played.

"Sir, I —"

"I know what Agent Spear promised you," Mr. Weathersky said. "It would be a shame to lose you, and I hope you'll stay with us when this is all over. But if not, I plan to honor your arrangement."

Ben felt suddenly furious. He was here because of the League. He was detached from his mom because of the League. And now Mr. Weathersky was making it sound like he was doing Ben some kind of favor to keep Agent Spear's promise and give him his life back.

"And, Ben," Mr. Weathersky said. "This mission may be the only way to make that happen."

That did it. Even through all his pain and fear and anger, Ben knew he had no choice.

"I'll do it," he said.

"Thank you, Ben," Mr. Weathersky said. "Your bravery and sacrifice are to be commended."

Shut up, Old One.

"Excellent," Ronin said. "Now let me out of here and let's get to work."

"I don't understand," Peter said, later that afternoon. "You're going on a mission with Ronin?"

"Looks that way," Ben said.

They were alone downstairs in the sleeping quarters, lying on their beds. After everything that had happened, Sasha had canceled their training for the day. Ben wondered if they'd cancel it altogether. Training seemed a little obsolete now.

"Why you?"

"Ronin asked for me."

"Yes, but why you?" Peter fidgeted one of his ankles. "It's because he saw you actuate, isn't it?"

"I don't know. Maybe."

"Does he know you need a Locus?"

Ben didn't want to deal with Peter's insecurity right now. "No . . . I don't know. . . . It didn't come up."

"When do you leave?"

"Soon. A couple of days."

Peter rolled onto his side, facing Ben. "I think you're the only real friend I've ever had."

Ben snorted. "Come on."

"No. Really." Peter was silent a few moments. "I wish I could help her."

"Who? Dr. Hughes?"

"Yeah." Peter's ankles came to rest. "Do you ever wonder about her?"

"Wonder what? If she's safe?"

"No. What it was all about for her. I'm pretty sure her research with us was illegal. Or at least unethical."

Ben scratched his chin. "You're probably right."

"So why'd she do it? She can't even actuate."

The answer seemed obvious to Ben. But when it came to other people, things that should have been obvious to Peter weren't. "I think all of us just want to make the world the way *we* want it to be. Even Dr. Hughes. And that's what actuation is."

Peter shrugged. "Maybe it's that simple."

"It's that simple," Ben said.

"I wish I could *really* make the world the way I want it to be."

"How would you change it?"

"I'd make myself smart enough that my dad would leave me alone."

"Why not change your dad so he doesn't care?"

"That would work, too." Peter slumped onto his back. "What about you?"

"I'd change my mom so she'd stick with something and let us stay in one place. From now on." Ben didn't want to talk about this anymore, and he got up from the bed.

They played some pool after that, and watched some TV, and spent the rest of the afternoon and evening trying not to talk about or think about what had happened the previous night. It was harder for Ben to not think about what lay ahead of him.

Ben didn't see much of Peter over the next couple of days. He had gone back to training with Sasha, while Ben spent his time with Agent Spear, Agent Taggart, and Ronin, preparing for the mission. Agent Spear drilled Ben on information about Poole and the Dread Cloaks. Agent Taggart rehearsed the things Ben would say and do. Ronin just hovered at the back of the room, listening and watching.

"And why do you want to defect?" Agent Taggart asked him for the hundred and fourteenth time.

Ben resisted rolling his eyes. "Look, I think I got this, okay?"

"No," Agent Taggart said. "Not okay. You head out tomorrow. And are you ready? Do you think you're prepared? Because once you're out there, we won't be around to save you like we did in that alley. You'll be on your own."

Agent Taggart still didn't get that she hadn't saved Ben, and neither had Agent Spear. But he let it go. "I'll be with Ronin."

"You'll be on your own. I don't care what kind of deal he made with Mr. Weathersky." Agent Taggart looked over her shoulder. "Don't trust him or count on him. Now tell me. Why do you want to defect?"

Ben sighed. "I hate authority and I don't like the Quantum League rules."

"Right."

"Wrong," Ronin said.

Agent Taggart spun around. "What do you mean, 'wrong'?"

"I've been listening to you people force-feed this poor kid scripts and answers for days. And as soon as we hit the field it'll be worth as much as a salt lick in a desert."

"Thank you for that," Agent Taggart said. "The input of a thief and a traitor."

Ronin shrugged.

"Don't listen to him, son," Agent Spear said. "You stick to the plan, now."

Ben nodded.

They gave him new clothes, and Ben made sure he took his Locus out of his old pocket. For the rest of that evening, he gripped it hard in his fist. He was doing this for his mom. He was doing it for Dr. Hughes. And maybe he was even doing it a little bit for Ronin. So he could see his daughter again.

Ben ate dinner that night with Peter and Sasha. They didn't say much, and when they did, it sounded forced. Sasha gave him a hug before he went downstairs to bed.

"Go get 'em, Locus Boy," she whispered in his ear.

He lay in bed awake most of the night, Peter and the others asleep all around him. All they faced the next day was more training. Ben finally nodded off. Woke up again. Slept some more. Then it was morning.

Time to go.

CHAPTER
13

HE wasn't hungry. He skipped breakfast and went straight up to the library; Peter came with him. Ben's fingers felt numb and icy, his palms wet. Agents Spear and Taggart were there, and so was Mr. Weathersky. They began talking to him. Ben guessed they were saying encouraging things; he wasn't really paying attention. But he nodded and said thank you, then Ronin came in.

"Car's out back," he said. "You ready?"

No.

"What?"

"Yes, sir."

Ronin chuckled. "Don't 'sir' me. You know my name."

"Okay . . . Ronin."

Ronin glanced around the room. "Don't look so nervous, people. I'll bring him back in one piece. I promise you that. And I'll get you your augmenter gun, too, along with one professor." He glared at Mr. Weathersky. "You just have my payment ready. You understand me?"

"Yes, Ethan," Mr. Weathersky said.

"Let's go, kid." Ronin left the room.

Ben stood where he was a moment longer, a little dazed, and then followed after him. The others accompanied him to the rear of the building. They stayed and watched as he climbed into the passenger seat of a car, beside Ronin. Peter waved to Ben as Ronin turned the ignition and popped the car into gear. Ben nodded back, and then forced himself to look away, to face the road ahead as Ronin pulled the car out into early morning traffic.

They drove in silence for a while. Ben's heartbeat slowed a little, and he gradually settled into his seat. He noticed the car for the first time. It was nice. New. Expensive.

"The League paid for this?"

"Are you kidding me? I couldn't be seen in a League piece of crap. I've got a reputation." Ronin stroked the steering wheel. "No, she's all mine."

"Nice," Ben said.

"Thanks."

"So tell me about yourself," Ronin said. "Who's not missing you?"

Ben looked out his side window. "My mom."

"Where is she?"

Ben stopped to think. What day was it? Then he checked the time, and figured out where she'd be. "On her way to class. Up at the university."

Ronin nodded. He flipped his blinker and made a sudden turn.

"Where are we going?" Ben asked.

"The university."

He sat up. "Why?"

"Look, I'm not going to lie to you, kid. What we're about to do is dangerous. Now, I meant what I said; I'll do everything I can to get you out of there safe. But just in case, for my own peace of mind, I'd like you to get another look at her before we go."

"You mean a last look," Ben said.

"I mean another look. That's all."

Ben's fear rushed back in. He closed his eyes and went quiet. He breathed deep and tried to slow down his heart. It was going to be okay. He'd see his mom, but he knew what to expect now. She wouldn't know him. Then he and Ronin would infiltrate the Dread Cloaks, save Dr. Hughes, get the augmenter gun, and go back to the League. Then Ben would get his life back.

Easy.

A few minutes later, they pulled through the main campus entrance.

"Which way?" Ronin asked.

Ben directed him to the building where his mom had her first class. Ronin pulled over, parked the car, and turned off the engine.

Ben checked the time. "We're early. She'll be here soon."

"All right." Ronin hit a button on the side of his seat. The back lowered with the hum of a motor. "Wake me up when you've seen her. It's too early for me." He folded his arms and closed his eyes.

Ben shook his head and watched the sidewalk fill up with students. He scanned faces, watching, waiting. The minutes ticked by. He wondered if he'd missed her, or gotten her schedule wrong, or if she were home sick.

Then he saw her. She strolled toward the building, and she was smiling. Then . . .

"No," Ben whispered.

Ronin's eyes snapped open. He sat up. "No, what? You see her?"

Ben pointed.

"That her?" Ronin asked. "She's pretty."

Ben looked out the opposite window. "Get me out of here. Now."

"Who's that guy with her?"

"NOW!"

"All right, all right." Ronin turned the key.

Ben couldn't resist looking one more time as they drove

away, just as Marshall opened the door for his mom and they went inside. Ben held his rage in a minute longer, and then he started kicking and punching the dash.

"Easy, easy!" Ronin reached his arm across Ben's chest and pressed him back into the seat. "Don't take it out on my car, kid."

Ben breathed hard. "Sorry."

Ronin held him a moment longer. "You good?"

Ben nodded, and Ronin released him.

Ben used his shirt to wipe the scuff marks his shoes had left on the dash. "Sorry."

"It's okay," Ronin said. "You wanna tell me what that was?"

"Not really."

"Okay, then."

Neither spoke for a while. Ben was grateful Ronin had let it go, because he didn't know what to say or think about what he'd just seen. Marshall. His mom. Her arm in his. She was smiling at him.

"You hungry?" Ronin asked. "How about some breakfast?"

"Sure," Ben said.

It wasn't like she hadn't dated before, and it wasn't because Ben didn't want her to date at all. He actually did, so long as she dated the right guy. But Marshall was *not* the right guy. This was one more thing in his life the League had screwed up.

Ronin took them to a small diner. "Best pancakes in the

city," he said. "They're sourdough. You ever had sourdough pancakes?"

Ben followed him inside. "I don't think so."

It was a seat-yourself kind of place, packed with old guys Ben guessed went there every day, sat at the same stool at the counter, and usually ordered the same thing. He and Ronin grabbed a corner booth, and when the waitress came, Ronin ordered sourdough pancakes for both of them and coffee for himself. Ben didn't care. He was even less hungry now than he had been before they left the League's headquarters.

While they waited for their food, Ronin propped both elbows on the table, letting his hands fall against each other over his coffee, and stared at Ben. "You want to know why I asked for you?"

Ben pulled his thoughts away from his mom. "You said I could play the part."

"Right, but do you know what I meant by that?"

"I guess not."

Ronin lifted his mug and sipped. "I could tell. I saw the way you looked at Mr. Weathersky, and I could tell."

"Tell what?"

"How angry you are. How much you hate the League."

"So?" Ben hadn't kept that a secret from anybody. "What does that have to do with this?"

Ronin leaned toward him. "Because when you look Poole in the eye and tell him how much you want to destroy the League, you won't have to act."

"That's not what Agent Taggart told me to sa —"

"Agent Taggart doesn't know what she's talking about. I've been doing this a long time, and one thing I've learned is that about five minutes into any undercover operation, there's a moment when you realize the script you thought you could rely on is completely worthless."

"So what should I do?"

"Improvise."

"Here you go, hon." The waitress appeared with their food, two stacks of pancakes so big they hung off the sides of the plates. "You let me know if you need anything else." She left the bill on the table.

Ronin peeled the wrappers off a couple of butters and smeared them over his pancakes. Then he poured on the syrup. "Eat 'em while they're hot, kid."

"I don't know if I can improvise," Ben said.

"You improvised in that alley just fine."

"You beat me."

"But that was your first real fight, and you were quick." Ronin folded a huge, dripping bite of pancake into his mouth.

Ben shook his head. He looked down at his plate and reached for the butter.

"But don't worry." Ronin wiped his mouth with a napkin. "You're not there for the fighting. Leave that to me. Your job, your *only* job, is to convince Poole that you want to spy for him." He rapped a knuckle on the table. "*That*, I know you can do."

Ben drizzled on the syrup and took a bite. The pancakes were really good. He'd have to come back here with his mom when . . . His body tensed up as it all came back. He wanted to pound the table.

"Whatever happened back there at the university," Ronin said. "Whatever's got you steaming. Is it the League's fault?"

"Yes."

"Then use it. Take what you're feeling and hold on to it. Bury it down deep so you can dig it up when you need it. You'll do just fine. Okay?"

Ben took a deep breath. "Okay."

"Good. Now finish your pancakes." He checked his watch. "We leave in ten."

"Where are we going?"

"To get the Paracelsus crew together."

Ben kept quiet until they were back in the car, well on their way. He didn't know where they were going, but this wasn't part of the plan. "Why are we getting your crew together?"

"This was never a two-man job," Ronin said. "But I wasn't about to let any agents mess it up. To work Poole, I need people I can count on."

Ben looked down at his lap. What could he do? He didn't have any way to contact the League. They'd said the Dread Cloaks would find anything like that when they searched him. Could he run? Maybe, but then what? They still didn't have any other way to rescue Dr. Hughes and get the aug-menter gun back.

"Look, kid," Ronin said. "You and I have two things in common. We both hate the Quantum League, and we both need something from them. This mission will get us both what we want, and I *will* see it done. You may not like how I go about it. The League sure won't. But it will get done. That's all I care about, and you are just gonna have to trust me."

He looked at Ben. Ben looked at Ronin's beaten and weathered face, and he believed him.

"Okay, Ronin. We'll do it your way."

"Okay. I'm glad that's settled." He pulled onto a side street and parked the car. "Now, there's an abandoned build-ing up ahead. It's my crew's safe house. When we go in there, the story is, you helped me escape."

"What?"

"They have to think the Dread Cloak mission is just another job. We're after that gun. For us. Not for the League. Got it?"

"Got it. We have to work your crew before your crew can work Poole."

Ronin grinned. "You're gonna do just fine, kid. Now, these are good people. They may look rough, but you don't have to worry about them."

"Okay."

They got out of the car and walked down the street. Ronin led them to what looked like an old warehouse. The windows were all boarded up at street level, and mostly broken out up above. He stuck a key in a padlock near the bottom corner of a heavy roll-up door, and then heaved it open a few feet.

"Go." He nodded Ben toward the opening, his eyes on the street.

Ben ducked inside, and Ronin followed him, letting the door fall shut behind them with a clang. The feeling of an actuation tingled the back of Ben's neck, and he turned to find Ronin kneeling on the ground, staring at the corner of the door.

He stood a moment later. "Just locking up from the outside. It's this way."

The warehouse was empty except for a few vehicles and a stack of old wooden pallets. They crossed to a door on the far side, which Ronin opened with a different key. He motioned for Ben to go through first, and then closed and locked the door behind them. They were in a narrow hallway, and Ben followed Ronin until they reached a corrugated metal stairway.

At the bottom they came to yet another door. This time, Ronin knocked. "Open up! It's me! And I've got a package."

Ben heard sounds on the other side. Then the door squealed open, revealing the largest man Ben had ever seen. He completely filled the doorway, and he didn't look soft. Ben couldn't guess how much of him was muscle underneath. He stared at them, his face as red and blank as a slab of beef.

"Out of the way, Polly," Ronin said.

The giant grunted and shambled aside.

"Let's go." Ronin guided Ben through the doorway.

They stopped a few steps into the room. Ben felt it. He knew Ronin felt it, too. Actuations, all ready to fire. The air buzzed with them. Ben didn't even dare look around.

"That's far enough," a voice said off to the side.

"What's this, Argus?" Ronin asked.

"You know what this is," the voice said. "We're doing what you would do if one of us showed up after getting nabbed. Move a muscle and we'll fry you."

"WE'RE alone," Ronin said. "Nobody followed us."

"Who's the kid?" That was a woman's voice, to the left.

"Ben," Ronin said. "He's a League recruit."

"Why'd you bring him here?" the first voice asked.

"I'll explain everything," Ronin said. "But it'll be easier if we cool things down a bit in here first."

A moment passed.

Ronin sighed. "Think about it. If I were a League rat, you guys'd already be trying to fight your way out of here. Now stand down."

Another moment passed.

Then the air calmed. The feeling of actuation dissipated, and Ben relaxed a little. There were two men on his right.

One of them was slender, wearing a leather jacket dripping with chains, and he had a six-inch mohawk. The other was stocky, and bushy. Bushy hair. Bushy eyebrows. Even a bushy sweater. The woman to Ben's left had blond hair cut to the length and line of her jaw, and she wore a business suit. The big guy, Polly, stood behind them blocking the door.

"That's better." Ronin scowled at them. "Have a seat, kid."

The room had a couple of sofas, sunken and stained. In one corner stood a little table with an expensive-looking coffeemaker, and nearby, a larger table rested in the light of three low-hanging bulbs, buried in papers and building plans. A whiteboard covered in half-erased scribbles took up most of one wall.

Ben went to one of the sofas and sat down slowly. Ronin collapsed onto the other, while the mohawk, the shrub, and the businesswoman took up positions around them.

"All right," the mohawk said. Ben recognized his voice as the one Ronin called Argus. "We've cooled it down. Now explain."

"I will," Ronin said. "But first, could you bring me a cup of coffee, Meg? I've still got the taste of that cheap League stuff in my mouth."

The woman's lips got so tight they disappeared. "When have I ever brought you coffee?"

"Fair enough." Ronin slapped his thighs. "Introductions. Ben, this is Argus, Megalesius, and Lykos. You already met Polyphemus as we came in."

"Introductions?" Argus said.

Ben didn't figure those were their real names. He wondered if they even knew one another's real names.

Ronin continued. "Meg and Lykos are the crew's firepower. Destruction specialists. Argus is our lookout, and he's pretty handy with a fog if we need cover. Polyphemus over there is our safecracker. You've never seen such delicate actuations."

The giant? Delicate? Was Ronin being sarcastic?

"As for me," Ronin said, "I round out the crew with strategy and logistics."

"I wish I knew the strategy behind what you're doing right now," Lykos said. "Who is the kid?"

"I already told you," Ronin said. "This is Ben."

"Not his name," Meg said. "What is he doing here?"

"I've got another job lined up," Ronin said. "And Ben is our inside man."

Argus took a seat, the chains on his coat jangling. "What kind of job?"

"A hustle with a smash and grab. And it's going to be hot."

"How hot?" Meg asked.

"*Everyone* will be coming after us," Ronin said. "And not just the League."

"Who's the mark?" she asked.

"Poole."

Argus chuckled. "Right."

Ronin paused. "I warned you it would be hot."

Argus stopped laughing. "Wait, you're serious?"

"What's the prize?" Meg asked.

"Well, that's where it gets interesting," Ronin said. "Seems some physicist has gone and made a portable augmenter."

Lykos stepped forward. "Did you say portable?"

Ronin nodded. "It's some kind of gun. Poole broke into the lab, stole the gun, and kidnapped the inventor."

The members of Ronin's crew grew quiet. Argus got up from the sofa and paced, staring at the floor. Meg and Lykos did the same. Polly stayed in the doorway. Ben wasn't even sure the giant was paying attention to the conversation. But Ronin clearly had the others intrigued.

"All right," Meg said. "How do we do this?"

Ronin stood and walked to the whiteboard. He erased an area and wrote Poole's name in the center. "The mark has been wanting a League agent in his pocket ever since he took over the Dread Cloaks. So far, he hasn't even come close. That's where the kid comes in." Ronin wrote down Ben's name, and drew an arrow pointing at Poole's. "For his own reasons, Ben here happens to hate the League as much as we do. That's why he helped me escape. But the League doesn't know that. They think I took him as a hostage."

Argus looked alarmed. "So they're after him? Right now?"

"Most likely," Ronin said. "But we have time."

"Time for what?" Meg asked.

Ronin pointed at the board. "I take Ben to Poole. We convince him that Ben wants to spy for him, and then we send Ben back to the League. Poole thinks he's a double agent, the League thinks he's theirs, but he's really *our* inside man for both."

"And then what?" Lykos asked.

Ronin stretched his neck. "I'm still working on that. I'll know more once Ben and I are in place with Poole."

The members of the crew cast doubtful looks among themselves. If they couldn't be convinced, then it would just be Ben and Ronin, and Ben saw the operation slipping away. Failing. *This was never a two-man job.* What could he do?

"This job is good." Ronin jabbed Poole's name with his marker. "You know me. Get me in there, and I'll find an angle."

"It's not you I'm worried about," Argus said.

He doubted Ben. They all did. Ben could see it. And why wouldn't they? Ronin was asking them to take on both the Quantum League and the Dread Cloaks when Ben was nothing more than a twelve-year-old recruit. He had to think of a way to convince them. They had to believe he was capable of doing this, that he was capable of anything. . . .

"But I will be with Ben," Ronin said. "I'll convince Poole."

Meg shook her head, her blond hair swinging. "This is too big, Ronin. The risks. I can't —"

"I thought you said we could count on them." Ben stood up. He felt the whole room shift its focus onto him. At that point, he wished he could take the words back. But he pointed at Ronin. "You told me I could trust you. That your crew could do the job."

Ronin blinked at him.

"Bunch of cowards," Ben said, listening to himself in disbelief at the same time. These were criminals. Just because Ronin had spared Ben didn't mean the rest of his crew would, no matter what Ronin had said about them. Ben forced himself to make eye contact with Argus, Meg, Lykos. He hoped they couldn't see his legs shaking.

"I'm going to Poole," Ben said. "And I am going to make the League pay for what they did to me. If you won't help me, there are other crews that will. I'm sure any one of them would love to get their hands on the augmenter gun."

Ben turned his back and marched toward the door. Toward Polly. This was it. *Capable of anything.* He looked up into the giant's face and said, "Out of my way."

Polly looked down at him, and then up at the rest of his crew, clearly baffled.

"Didn't you hear me?" Ben gripped his Locus. This was probably the dumbest thing he had ever done, but he couldn't turn back. "OUT OF MY WAY!"

Polly frowned.

Ben closed his eyes, rustled up a mess of electrons, and let them fly. It wasn't a powerful lightning bolt, not enough to kill, but it knocked the giant off his feet and got the room up in a frenzy. Ben felt actuations blazing up behind him. *Definitely* the dumbest thing he had ever done. He spun around to face the rest of the crew.

They all looked ready to kill him, but Ronin rushed in between Ben and the others, waving his arms. "Hold your fire!"

"Who *is* this kid?!" Argus shouted.

"I'm the kid who *was* going to be your inside man," Ben said.

Then he heard a deep rumble behind him. Ben looked over his shoulder as Polly lumbered to his feet, rubbing his head with his big, meaty hands. This guy didn't need an actuation to kill someone. Ben wanted to run, right past the giant, up the stairs, and out of the warehouse. But he braced himself and held his ground.

Polly stepped up and looked down, past the scorch mark on his shirt, straight at Ben.

"Polly?" Ronin said. "Polly, stay — stay calm, now."

Ben looked right back up at the giant, and hoped his voice would come out sounding stronger than he felt. "You want another one, big boy?"

Polly looked at Ronin, his face as blank as it had been before. "I'm in."

• • •

After that, the rest of the crew threw in, too. From their wary glances in his direction, Ben suspected they were now wondering about his sanity, and to be honest, so was he. The shaking only got worse after he sat down again and replayed what he had done in his mind. It could, and probably should, have ended very differently. But afterward, Ronin grinned at him in a way that almost looked . . . proud.

They spent the next few hours planning, Ronin at the whiteboard, trying out idea after idea, but they never settled on one. The coffeemaker popped and gurgled and hissed continuously. The sofa got tired and loose under Ben. The whiteboard became an unreadable tangle of marker.

"The problem," Meg said, "is that a job like this needs months of groundwork, not hours or days. Preparation, preparation, preparation. Isn't that what you always say, Ronin?"

"It is. But we don't have months."

"We need more time," Argus said.

"Look, we'll have time once Ben is inside." Ronin went for another cup of coffee. "Right now, we just need to get him there. That's it. We're making this more complicated than it has to be."

"We've run all the angles." Lykos stood and walked to the board. "Nothing works. Poole may be crazy, but he's no idiot. Ben can't just walk in and volunteer. Poole would see through that. We could stage a situation where Ben gets caught and flips, but Poole wouldn't trust that very far. Not far enough, anyway. He'd think Ben was just trying to save his own skin."

"If we had time," Meg said, "we could salt the mine. Ben could drop a few crumbs, give Poole a little taste, then reel him in."

"Listen to me," Ronin said. "No. Time."

"Then I think we should scrap it." Argus lifted both arms and let them fall against his legs. Then he looked at Ben, and his smile was uneasy. "I mean, sorry, kid. We tried."

"We're not scrapping it." Everyone turned to look at Polly. He stood in a corner of the room, pointing a beef rib of a finger at Ben. "We got the kid. That's the most important part. Just get him in there."

"We're trying, Polly," Argus said. "But maybe —"

"We've got the kid," Ronin whispered. He looked at Polly. "That's it."

"What's it?" Meg asked.

"A fiddle game," Ronin said.

No one in the crew spoke. But gradually their eyes all lit up. They smiled and nodded to one another.

"What's a fiddle game?" Ben asked.

"That'll do it," Lykos said. "Poole will buy it."

"What will he buy?" Ben raised his voice. "What's a fiddle game?"

"The setup won't be too difficult," Meg said. "We just have to get Poole's attention."

Ronin smirked. "I know how to do that."

"Stop!" Ben jumped up, surprising everyone in the room. Argus actually flinched next to him. "Would somebody please tell me what a fiddle game is?"

CHAPTER
15

THE next night, the Paracelsus crew stood across the street from an ordinary brick building in the shadows of a park. Two men, Dread Cloaks, guarded the door. Ben didn't feel as nervous as he thought he would. Maybe it was because this seemed easy compared to shooting a lightning bolt at Polly. Maybe he was feeling a safety-in-numbers thing with the crew. Or maybe he was just getting used to this.

"That's it?" Argus asked. "That's where he keeps it?"

Ronin looked up at the building. "Some of it."

"And you're sure this will get his attention?" Lykos asked.

"Oh yeah," Ronin said. "This'll do it."

"Then what are we waiting for?" Meg asked.

"Right." Ronin turned to face them all. "Remember, this can't seem too easy, but we can't have any casualties, either. We can't put Poole in a situation where he'll lose face in front of the gang."

"We got it," Polly said. "Simple fiddle game."

The fiddle game was a con. The way they'd explained it to Ben, a guy goes into a restaurant carrying a fiddle, orders food, eats, and then claims he can't pay because he left his wallet somewhere else. So he offers to leave his fiddle behind as collateral while he goes to get his money. The restaurant owner agrees, and the guy leaves. After that, a second guy, who's in on the game, comes up and tells the restaurant owner that the fiddle is special, it's worth a lot of money, and he wants to buy it. Then, all of a sudden, the second guy has to go to an appointment or something, but he leaves his business card behind. So now the restaurant owner starts thinking he's got something really valuable on his hands, this fiddle, and when the owner of the instrument comes back, the restaurant owner offers to buy it. The guy says he couldn't possibly part with it, it's his livelihood, so the restaurant owner offers more money, knowing he can make it back when he sells it. They haggle, and finally agree on a price, and the fiddle owner leaves with the money. Trouble is, when the restaurant owner goes to call the fake buyer, he can't find him. The two guys split the money, and the restaurant owner is left with a piece-of-crap fiddle.

In the game they were about to run with Poole, Ben was the fiddle. But he didn't take it personally.

"All right." Ronin turned to Ben. "You ready?"

"Yes," Ben said. Even if he wasn't, he still had to make sure he looked and sounded like that crazy kid who could do anything.

"Are you?" Meg asked. "Are you sure this will work?"

"Relax," Ronin said. "I know Poole. He'd have to be pretty paranoid not to fall for it. Now, let's go."

The crew broke apart and scattered in different directions. Argus stayed in the park, and Ben felt him actuating in the darkness behind them. Moments later, a fog rolled in and settled in front of the building. It turned the two Dread Cloaks into hazy shadows, but they were agitated shadows. They could tell the fog was an actuation. That was the plan.

Lykos and Meg rushed from their positions into the mist.

"Steady." Ronin's voice carried through all their earpieces. "Let them call it in first."

The Dread Cloaks came together, forming one shadow. They whispered to one another, but then one of them raised his voice a little. He had to if he wanted to be heard, because he was on his phone.

"We've got company," he said. "Tell Poole."

"Now," Ronin said.

Two lights flashed inside the fog, two lightning bolts, and the Dread Cloak shadows slumped to the ground.

Ben heard Lykos in his earpiece. "They're dead."

Ronin's eyes widened. "WHAT?"

"Kidding," Lykos said. "But they're out cold. Polly's up."

The giant lumbered forward, followed by Ronin and Ben. They met up with Meg and Lykos in the fog, over the unconscious bodies of the two guards. Meg made a sweeping gesture from Polly toward the door.

"After you."

Polly interlocked his fingers and popped all his knuckles at once. He strode up to the door, and Ben moved to where he could get a good look. He'd been waiting to see this. He expected the giant to rip the door off its hinges with an actuation or something. But instead, Polly just knelt down in front of it. He hunched his broad shoulders over the lock, brought his hands up close to his chest, and then his big fingers started flicking and dancing. Ben felt tiny actuations, little tickles, almost unnoticeable. They lasted a moment. Then the lock clicked, and the door popped open.

That was it? Ben looked at Ronin.

"Told you. Delicate." Ronin winked. "Polly here knows just about every lock there is, inside and out."

Polly heaved himself to his feet. "Electronic locks give me fits, though."

"You've got most of them down," Ronin said.

"Yes, yes," Meg said. "But Poole is supposed to catch us in the act of actually doing something, isn't he?"

"Right." Ronin turned toward the park. "You can head on out, Argus."

"I think I'll stay and watch the show," came his reply in Ben's ear. "If you don't mind."

"Suit yourself." Ronin led them into the building.

They ran into a few more Dread Cloaks, but Lykos and Meg were too fast for them, faster than any Actuators Ben had seen. Ronin led them to an elevator, pressed the button, and they waited. And waited. All of them watched the little floor numbers changing above the doors. Then the elevator dinged, and they all squeezed in, including Polly.

They were heading up to a keyed floor, so Polly went to work with his delicate actuations, and soon the elevator dinged again.

They rode it up, and when the elevator stopped, the doors opened onto what looked like a museum. The crew spilled out, and for a minute they all just stared. Across the open space, spotlights bathed dozens of marble statues in white, while angled ceiling lights shone on paintings hanging on the walls. There were even a few tall glass cases filled with wooden artifacts and clothing, baskets and rugs.

"I told you," Ronin said. "Poole has a thing for art."

Ben actually recognized some of the pieces from schoolbooks and TV, or at least some of the artists.

"I don't understand," Lykos said. "Why doesn't he keep this more secure?"

"Because who would be stupid enough to steal from Poole?" Meg said.

Ben knew the answer to that.

"Ronin." Argus spoke in Ben's earpiece again. "He's here."

And they were about to find out just how stupid they were.

"This is it," Ronin said. "Make it convincing, but nobody gets killed, all right? Do like I told you. Ben, stick with me. The rest of you, fan out."

The crew took up positions behind the larger statues and the glass cases, facing the elevator. Ben and Ronin crouched behind a big copper sculpture of what looked like abstract flames. It sounded hollow when Ben knocked on it.

"Don't do that," Ronin said.

They waited. And waited. Once again watching the little numbers above the doors.

"This is the slowest elevator in the city," Meg said.

A few minutes later, the doors opened, and a group of Dread Cloaks got off. They all wore the same thing they'd worn in Dr. Hughes's lab. Black vests with red shirts. Only they didn't have the ski masks on. Ben wondered which of them was Poole.

"Now!" Ronin shouted.

He unleashed a fireball. Ice and lightning flew from Lykos, Meg, and Polly. Ben got off a lightning bolt of his own as the Dread Cloaks ran for cover, returning fire. Two statues shattered in the first volley, and one painting went up in flames. And just like Ronin had predicted, that was all it took.

"Hold your fire!" one of the Dread Cloaks screamed. "Hold your fire!"

"Hold!" Ronin shouted from behind the sculpture.

"I don't know who you are!" the Dread Cloak said, and Ben recognized him. Poole. "But if one more piece of art is damaged, your death will not be an easy one!"

"Poole?" Ronin said. "Is that you?"

"Who is speaking?" Poole asked.

"Ronin! It's Ronin."

Silence.

"Is this all yours?" Ronin asked. "This your art?"

"All of it," Poole said.

"Wow," Ronin said. "I'm impressed. You've come a long way since our days on the True Coat crew."

"And you have fallen far to steal from me," Poole said.

"Steal from you?" Ronin said. "I'd never steal from you. I had no idea —"

"Not even as you took out my guards?"

Ronin laughed. "I didn't even notice. You know me. Shoot first."

Silence.

"So, uh, listen, Poole. What are we gonna to do here?"

"I'm going to wait until you try to leave this building, and then I'm going to kill your entire crew."

Ronin looked at Ben, and Ben couldn't tell from his expression if this was going well or not.

"That's one way of doing it," Ronin said. "I suppose. But I was kind of hoping our time together might be worth something. I seem to remember pulling you out of a jam or two. Like that job in Cairo, remember?"

No response.

"Come on," Ronin said. "This is just a simple misunderstanding."

Still no response.

"Look, I don't like doing this from behind this sculpture. I'm coming out. Don't shoot."

Ronin waited a moment, and then slowly, one hesitant inch at a time, he stepped out from behind the copper flames with his hands in the air. Ben didn't breathe. They could kill him instantly.

Ronin nodded toward the sculpture. "You like this modern crap?"

"Watch your words," Poole said. "Men have died for their taste in art."

"What men?" Ronin asked.

"Men from whom I stole it."

"Ah," Ronin said. "Well, nothing's been stolen here. No one else needs to die for art. I don't see why we can't come to an understanding."

"Can't do that, Ronin," Poole said. "Even for old times' sake. You've crossed a line."

"Have I?" Ronin asked. "Ask yourself, have I? Have I killed a Dread Cloak?"

"No."

"Have I stolen anything from you? Yet?"

"Not yet."

"All right, then, no foul. So what's the problem?"

Poole didn't answer him. Ronin was threading that loophole in the gangster's honor that might allow them to move on to the next step of the game.

"Look," Ronin said. "How about this. I'll pay you for the art we destroyed. I'll even throw in some for that painting over there, which I'm pretty sure was your guys. Will that settle us?"

"I suppose we might reach a compromise. For the sake of our past association."

"Great," Ronin said. "Let's talk price —"

"Three million," Poole said. "One million, each."

Ronin guffawed. "Come on."

"One million each."

"Really? No discount for size?" Ronin pointed at the smallest of the broken statues.

"They had . . . sentimental value," Poole said. "Hard to put a price on that. Easier for you to put a price on the lives of your crew, I imagine. Three million to buy their way out of here."

Ronin scratched his head. He paced a step or two back and forth. "Three million. Three million? Three million."

"I grow impatient," Poole said. "Do you have it?"

"Of course I have it," Ronin said. "But this is gonna break me."

"Not my problem," Poole said. "And you've got five seconds more. Then I take back my offer."

"Okay, okay." Ronin sighed. "Three million. But you know I don't have it with me."

"And what?" Poole said. "You'll just pop off and go get it? Promise to come back and all that?"

"Something like that," Ronin said.

"Call out your crew," Poole said.

"What?"

"Call out your crew!"

Ronin hesitated. "Come on out, all of you. It's okay. We've almost got a deal."

Polly, Meg, and Lykos all stepped out from behind their hiding places. Ben stayed where he was. Poole couldn't see him yet. He couldn't recognize him too early in the game.

"Some familiar faces," Poole said. "Listen up, all of you, 'cause here's what I'm thinking, and I'm leaving the decision up to you. I let Ronin go to fetch my money. You all stay here. Ronin doesn't come back, you all die. Understand?"

The three looked at Ronin, then at one another.

"So yea or nay?" Poole said. "That sound good to you? You trust Ronin here with your lives? Let's have an election. Two out of three carries the day."

"I trust him," Meg said.

"No way," Lykos said.

Polly turned to Ronin. "You coming back, boss? You swear?"

"I swear," Ronin said.

"Don't be an idiot, Polly," Lykos said.

But Polly turned to Poole. "I say yes."

Poole raised an eyebrow. "I'm impressed by the loyalty of your crew. All right, Ronin. You're free to go. You have one hour."

Ben peeked around the sculpture as Poole's men cleared a path.

Ronin took a deep breath. "Right." He walked to the elevator and pressed the button. He waited. And waited. At one point, he turned around, smiled. Then the doors opened and he got on. "Don't worry," he said to his crew. "I'll be back." The doors closed.

"You three," Poole said. "Stay right where you are. We'll just sit tight as we are."

Lykos turned to Meg and Polly. "You're both out of your minds. He isn't coming back."

CHAPTER
16

THIRTY minutes passed, during which no one talked. Lykos and Meg had sat down on the floor. Polly just stood there. At the end of the room by the elevator, Poole's men whispered and joked among themselves, but Poole never said a word. Ben kept to his hiding place, safe behind the big sculpture, undiscovered.

Forty-five minutes in, Lykos stood up. He fidgeted. He paced. "He's not coming back. I told you."

"Sit down," Meg said. "He's coming."

Lykos checked his watch. "He should have been back by now."

That was Ben's cue. He was supposed to make a noise. Something that drew attention, but not something obvious, like a sneeze. Poole's museum had a cement floor, with a thick glossy seal over it. Ben dragged the toe of his shoe across it, and made a little squeak.

"What was that?" Poole asked.

Ben squeezed his eyes shut for a second, waiting. Then Poole came around the statue and looked down at him. His face, not hidden this time, was lean and sunken around his eyes and his cheeks.

"Well, this is unexpected," he said. "And just who are you?"

"He's no one," Polly said.

"No one?" Poole reached down, grabbed Ben's arm, and yanked him to his feet hard enough that Ben felt a wrenching in his shoulder. He was stronger than Ben had expected, and Poole dragged him out into the open. "This looks like a very real someone to me."

"Leave him alone," Meg said. "He's just a kid."

"But a kid on your crew, apparently." Poole still had Ben by the arm. "Which makes me doubt he's *just* anything." He looked at Ben, his eyes the same blue Ben had seen through the ski mask. "Wait. I know you."

Ben looked down at the ground. "I don't think so."

"No, I definitely know you." He released Ben's arm. "Devilish tricks. Devilish tricks in a child's playpen."

Ben looked up. "Yeah, all right. That was me. So what?"

Poole smiled. "Still defiant."

"Leave the kid alone," Polly said.

"Or what?" Poole asked.

"Or I'll kill you," Polly said.

The Dread Cloaks stirred. Poole's smile fell. "You aren't in a position to make threats."

"Not a threat," Polly said.

Even though Ben knew they were playing their roles, something in the way Polly said it felt genuine. Like the big guy really had his back. Poole took a step toward the giant, and Ben felt actuations stirring among his Dread Cloaks.

"Wait." Meg slid in front of Polly. "Just wait, Poole. He doesn't mean that." She put her hands on Polly's arms and looked up into his face. "Just sit tight. Ronin will be back any minute."

"No, he won't," Lykos said. "Hour's almost up."

"Then too bad for you." Poole looked back at Ben. "All of you."

"Unless we can come to a deal of our own," Lykos said.

"You carry three million around on your person?" Poole asked.

"No," Lykos said. "But we have something a lot more valuable than that right here in this room. Ronin left it with you, and you didn't even know it."

"And what might that be?" Poole asked.

Lykos pointed at Ben. "The kid."

"The kid?" Poole cocked his head at Ben. "Yes, I think it's time to find out just who you are. How is it I found you in that university laboratory weeks ago, and now find you here with the Paracelsus crew in my art collection?"

Ben shrugged. "Coincidence."

"Don't talk, Ben," Meg said.

"Ben?" Poole came closer. "All right, then. Ben. Don't listen to her, Ben. Talk. Tell me. I want to know."

"I'll tell you," Lykos said. "Ben is Ronin's inside man with the League. After your little raid on that laboratory, the League recruited him, and then Ronin got his hands on him."

"Is this true?" Poole asked Ben. "Are you in the League?"

"Yes," Ben said.

"He's a prodigy," Lykos said. "The Old One said so himself."

"Are you a prodigy, Ben?" Poole asked.

"Yes."

Poole nodded. "I like your confidence. And are you Ronin's man on the inside?"

"No."

"No?" Poole glanced at Lykos with a questioning look.

"I'm nobody's man," Ben said. "I work for myself. Right now, it happens to suit my interests to feed intel to Ronin."

"Your —" Poole chuckled. "Pardon me, but your interests? And what might those be?"

This was the moment for Ben to tell the truth. This was the moment to dig up his rage and let it show. He thought of

Marshall, and he glowered. "I want to make the League pay for what they did to me."

"Is that so?"

"Yes." Ben felt the anger, the real anger, the deep anger, bubbling up hot, threatening to geyser. "After you busted up the lab, they took me. They detached me. They ruined my life, and I'm going to do everything I can to ruin theirs. From the inside."

Poole didn't say anything. He just looked at Ben another moment, and then turned to Lykos. "You're right. This is more valuable."

"So how about we make a deal," Lykos said. "You let us go and keep the kid. Consider our debt paid."

"Traitor!" Polly lunged at Lykos and decked him. Hard. Ben winced as Lykos sprawled on the ground. He'd insisted the hit had to be real, and Polly had reluctantly agreed.

"Polly, stop!" Meg shouted, tugging on one of the giant's arms.

Polly looked down at her and grunted. Lykos slid away from him along the floor until he was a safe distance away, and then he staggered to his feet, rubbing his rapidly swelling jaw.

"And what would I do with the kid?" Poole asked, as if the whole thing hadn't happened.

"Whatever you want," Lykos said. "I really don't care. I just want to get out of here and forget this whole thing happened."

Poole checked his watch. "Hour's well up. Ronin is a marked man. We'll run him down by morning. As for the rest of you, I will take your inside man and consider him payment in full. Now get out of here."

This was the part Ben had dreaded, the only part of the plan that had worried him. His breathing quickened as he watched the rest of the crew move to the elevator, and his stomach clenched up as they got inside it. The doors closed, and then he was alone with Poole. It wouldn't be for long; he knew Ronin was coming. But he still felt alone and afraid.

"What an unexpected night this has turned out to be." Poole looked at the shattered statues and then at Ben. "What kind of intel do you feed to Ronin?"

"Whatever I can get my hands on."

"How useful could that be, at your age?"

"I'm not a full agent yet," Ben said. "But my reputation as a prodigy means people tend to talk around me. I overhear things."

"What kinds of things?"

Ben shrugged. He wasn't supposed to give Poole anything. The plan was to get him curious, and then Ronin would close the deal. "Just things."

"Look around you, devilish boy." Poole took Ben's chin in his hand and lifted it. "Do you see a friendly face? Where is your crew? They abandoned you. So did Ronin. Just whose man do you think you are now?"

"Same as when I walked in," Ben said. "My own."

Poole punched him in the gut. Ben doubled over, gasping, clutching his stomach. He dropped to his knees. That wasn't supposed to happen. That was not part of the plan, and Poole could hurt him a lot worse. Poole could kill him. Where was Ronin?

"You see now, don't you?" Poole said. "Whose man you are. So I'll ask you again. What kinds of things do you overhear?"

Ben rubbed his stomach. He had to answer him. He had to give him something. He feared what Poole would do if he didn't. But what should he say?

Improvise. He reached for the first thing that came to his mind.

"I know —" He struggled to speak, his breath still coming back. "I know they're planning a raid . . . to rescue that professor and steal the portable augmenter."

Poole jerked upright.

Ben realized then what he'd just done. He'd blown it. The whole job. He'd tipped their hand and made Poole think about the very thing he *wasn't* supposed to think about. Ben felt like throwing up.

"When?" Poole asked.

When? "A week from tomorrow." Why had he said that? *Still blowing it.*

"How many agents will there be?"

"I . . ." *Shut up, Ben.* "I don't know."

"Will it be a night raid?"

"I don't know."

"What about —?"

"He's back," one of the Dread Cloaks said, holding a radio to his ear. "Ronin is back. He's coming up."

Ben worked hard to keep the relief from showing on his face.

Poole turned from him toward the elevators. "An unexpected night."

A few moments later, the elevator dinged, and Ronin walked off. He looked at Poole, then at Ben, then around the room. "Where's my crew?"

"You failed them," Poole said. "So we came to terms."

"What terms?" Ronin asked.

Poole said nothing. Then he nodded toward Ben. "Quite a prize, a League recruit in your pocket."

Ronin's eyes narrowed. "Comes in handy. You all right, Ben?"

Ben got to his feet. "Yes."

"What terms?" Ronin asked Poole.

"Do you have my money?" Poole asked.

"Here's the thing," Ronin said. "I've got some of it, but I can get you the rest."

"No, *here's* the thing," Poole said. "We made a deal. If you can't pay, your life is forfeit."

"But I can pay, I just need —"

"I know you can pay," Poole said. "But not with money."

"Then how?"

Poole put a hand on Ben's shoulder, and out of reflex, Ben threw it off. "Don't touch me."

"Easy, now," Poole said.

"Come on, Poole." Ronin took several steps toward them, farther into the museum. "He's just a kid."

Poole said nothing.

"So these were the terms?" Ronin asked. "My crew gave up Ben to save themselves?"

"Honor among thieves, eh?" Poole stepped toward Ronin. His Dread Cloaks closed in behind, cutting off access to the elevator. "That's all done with. Which means you and I still need to settle up."

"It doesn't need to go down like this," Ronin said.

The moment had come. So far, Poole had played right into the fiddle game, but this was the final gamble. Ben felt actuations building, the Dread Cloaks heating up. If Poole gave the order, Ronin would be dead, instantly. He had to close the deal now.

"Let's just take it easy." Ronin raised both his hands. "What if I come work for you? I'll pay off my debt doing jobs for you. You've seen me in action. You know what I can do."

Poole seemed to be thinking that over.

Ben wished he could do something to convince him. He thought back to Mr. Weathersky, the way he had influenced people, somehow nudging them toward loyalty or fear. Like a kind of actuation. How had he done that?

Finally, Poole sighed. "Ronin, I respect your abilities, I do. But I can't have you work for me. I'd never be able to turn my back. And if I cut you loose now, there'll be blowback, I have no doubt."

That wasn't what he was supposed to say. He was supposed to agree. Ronin had sworn he knew Poole, and Poole would agree.

"Poole, you — you're sounding paranoid." Ronin's voice cracked a little. "You've changed since our True Coat days. You know me. How many jobs did we do together?"

"All in the past," Poole said. "Good-bye, Ronin."

Ronin looked at Ben, his eyes wild, but not with fear. He seemed to be frantically searching for a way out, a solution, an angle.

Poole turned to his men. "On my mark." They shifted on their feet, a firing squad. This was an execution.

Ronin shook his head. "Poole, wait —"

Poole took a breath. "Three, two —"

"STOP!" Ben shouted.

Poole, the Dread Cloaks, Ronin, all turned toward him.

How had Mr. Weathersky done it? Actuations began with thoughts, consciousness reaching out, creating reality. What if Ben's consciousness could reach out to affect another?

"You do *not* want to do that," Ben said.

Fear. They needed to feel fear.

"Why not?" Poole asked.

"Trust me." Ben thought of heart rates rising. He thought of cold palms and trembling hands. He thought of chills along the spine, the hollow of dread in the chest. Ben gripped his Locus and pushed fear outward, imagining waves of it crashing over the minds of Poole and the others. "You kill Ronin, and you'll regret it."

One of Poole's blue eyes twitched. "How?"

"You're going to need him when the League raids you next week. He knows their tactics. He knows the agents by name. He knows their strengths and weaknesses. Without him, it doesn't matter if I'm your inside man or not. The League will still take you down."

Poole swallowed. Ben couldn't believe it. It seemed to be working. He held the Locus tighter.

Fear.

"Perhaps," Poole said, "I am being rash. Perhaps you both might be of use to me."

"There's no perhaps," Ben said. "Now, call off your men."

Poole stared at Ben for a long time. Ben stared back, radiating the way Mr. Weathersky had, and it was Poole who looked away first.

He turned to the Dread Cloaks. "Power down."

CHAPTER
17

THEY rode in silence, surrounded by Dread Cloaks. The van coasted down empty, sleeping streets, reminding Ben of the night drive he'd taken with the League to catch Ronin in the first place. It almost felt like that had been a different him than the Ben in this van now. Since that night, he'd faced down criminals and a gang lord. He'd been a member of a heist crew, and now he was officially undercover in the Dread Cloaks.

Each of those steps had brought him closer to the goal. Get Dr. Hughes and the augmenter gun for the League, then get his life back.

He wondered where the van was going. Probably not

anywhere near Dr. Hughes. Poole would have her locked up tight somewhere. Ben hoped she was all right.

Eventually, they left downtown and headed out on the highway (or interstate?) toward an industrial part of the city.

"Where are we going?" Ronin asked.

No one answered him.

They took a freeway exit near a sprawling refinery. Bright lights traced the outlines of its buildings, catwalks, and pipes, and the smell of rotten eggs clung to the air around it. At the far end, two identical brick smokestacks rose from a windowless fortress, belching twin flames into the night.

After the refinery, the van turned onto a road that carried them into a derelict suburb. Nearly every house looked abandoned, with dead lawns, broken or boarded-up windows, graffiti, and sagging roofs.

Soon, the streets turned from residential to business. They passed strips of empty and anonymous storefronts and offices, the ghosts of their former logos peeking out from behind FOR SALE banners. After a few blocks of this, the van turned onto a wide, paved entrance, and they passed under an arched sign.

Ben read it and leaned in close to Ronin. "Mercer Beach? Where's the ocean?"

"It's an amusement park," Ronin said. "Or was. They shut it down years ago."

What are we doing at an amusement park?

The van cut straight across a vast parking lot, avoiding a few fallen lampposts. Those still standing were dark and lifeless, weeds shooting up through cracks in the asphalt at their feet. The van swung past the main gate, the ticket booths with their red-and-white-striped canopies, and continued alongside the park's chain-link fence to a rear entrance. A sign hanging on it still read DELIVERY VEHICLES ONLY.

The driver of their van honked.

Two Dread Cloaks swung the gate inward, and the van pulled through, then took a winding road around the backside of the park. The silhouettes of a Ferris wheel and a carousel rose up against the night sky over the backs of smaller booths and buildings. Beyond those, the refinery smokestacks burned, not too far away. No wonder they'd shut this place down.

The van eventually stopped at a loading dock, and everyone piled out behind a building that had been made to look like a giant circus tent. Poole led the way up a flight of cement steps and through the building's rear entrance. Inside, they seemed to be behind some kind of stage, and from there they followed Poole down a hallway where the doors all had glittery stars on them, with nameplates like MADAME CHANDELIER, PIPSQUEAK THE CLOWN, and SIMON NIGHTSPELL.

Poole opened a door labeled KARL TITAN. "Inside, both of you."

Ben and Ronin entered the room, and the door shut behind them. They heard a key in the lock, and footsteps leading away. But two swinging blades of shadow coming in under the door said Poole had left guards just outside.

The room was empty, except for a couple of chairs, and a vanity with a large mirror bordered by lightbulbs. Ronin ushered them away from the door, into a corner.

"What now?" Ben whispered.

"We wait for Poole to decide what he wants to do with us. My guess, he'll want to get you back to the League soon to find out about this raid. How come you didn't tell me about that before?"

"Because there is no raid. I made it up."

Ronin gave his head a quick shake. "What? Why would you make that up?"

"I was improvising, okay? And don't forget that my improvising saved your life."

"Yes, it did," Ronin said. "But you also put us on a pretty tight timetable. One week, you said?"

Ben nodded.

"So we have one week to find Dr. Hughes and the portable augmenter. And then the League is supposedly staging a raid on the Dread Cloaks?"

Ben nodded again.

"Then your job just got a lot tougher, kid."

"How?"

"You might have to convince the Quantum League to stage an actual raid."

• • •

They stayed in the dressing room for what felt like a couple of hours, and then a Dread Cloak came for them. They followed him back down the hallway, to the backstage area. From there, they climbed a staircase attached to the wall, till they were up high among the lights and the rigging, and Ben could look down on the other side of the backdrop.

The building was an arena, part-circus, part-theater, with a sawdust performance ring in front of the raised stage. It was the kind of place his mom probably would have brought him for his birthday when he was younger.

They reached the top of the stairs, where a network of catwalks crisscrossed away from them out over the whole arena.

"This way," the Dread Cloak said, and he led them along a walkway to what looked like some kind of control room.

"Poole's office, I take it?" Ronin asked.

"Yes," the Dread Cloak said.

They reached the door, the Dread Cloak knocked, and a voice said to enter.

Inside, Poole sat at a desk before a wall of windows that offered a view of the entire audience and stage far below. Behind him, a vast and complicated panel bore hundreds of switches and dials, Ben assumed for all the lights and sounds in the building.

Two armchairs sat in front of Poole's desk, facing him,

and behind those chairs stood three more Dread Cloaks. One of them, a guy with red hair, stared hard at Ben.

"Gentlemen." Poole gestured to the chairs. "Make yourselves comfortable."

And the chairs were comfortable, even though Ben could feel the redhead still glaring at the back of his neck.

"Nice place you got here," Ronin said. "Gives new meaning to high and mighty."

"It suits my need for privacy," Poole said. "Speaking of which, the rest of you are dismissed."

The Dread Cloaks filed from the room, and the redhead shot Ben one last look before he shut the door behind them. Ben could feel and hear their footsteps on the stairs going back down. Ronin kept one ear cocked to the sound until it faded.

And then he said, "Okay, Poole. Now tell me what you're doing all the way out here."

"What do you mean?" Poole asked.

"How can you run the Dread Cloaks so far from your turf?"

"I don't need to be there in person to run the show."

"Yes, you do. I couldn't run a crew from here, let alone a street gang." Ronin spread his arms and looked around the room. "I don't mean to be rude, but this is weird."

Poole's sunken eyes turned hard.

"You *have* gotten paranoid, haven't you?" Ronin said. "There's something going on here. Something's got you spooked."

Ben remembered Ronin saying the same thing to Mr. Weathersky. Getting spooked seemed to be going around.

"Yes," Poole said quietly.

"Pardon?" Ronin leaned forward in the armchair. "Yes, what?"

"Yes." Poole spoke louder. "Something has me . . . on edge."

"What?"

Poole stood. He clasped his hands behind his back and turned away from them, facing the windows. "You know most Dread Cloaks are only Class One Actuators, don't you?"

Ronin shrugged. "Sure."

"Thugs. Petty, simple, blunt instruments. When I took over, it was easy for a while. They feared me. I'd shown them what I could do, and that was enough to keep them in line. But inevitably, rivals started coming up through the ranks, and I put a few of them down. Dramatically. Terribly. Examples had to be made to stem the tide."

"But there's somebody new, isn't there?" Ronin asked. "Somebody who's got you running scared. That's why you're out here. Are you still in control?"

Poole pivoted to look at them. "Yes."

"Who is it?"

"I haven't been able to identify him." He sat back down at his desk. "But rumors reach my ears. They say he can actuate Class Threes. More and more Dread Cloaks throw in with him every day. I'm hemorrhaging."

"So what do you want from us?" Ronin asked.

Poole looked at Ben. "This raid. If I stop it, if I defeat the League, *me*, the show of force will staunch the bleeding. The Dread Cloaks will see that *I*" — he pounded his chest — "am in charge. I'll starve out this pretender to my throne."

Ben tried to look and sound like the kid he'd become in the Paracelsus crew safe house. The one capable of anything. "I can do something about that."

"I need you to get me everything you can on this raid," Poole said. "When. Where. How many agents. Which agents. Their strategy. All of it. You have two days."

"Done," Ben said. "But I'll need Ronin and his crew to help me."

"Yes, fine." Poole slipped a phone out of his vest pocket. "We're done here. I'll have someone drive you back into the city now. Go."

Ben and Ronin rose to leave, but as they reached the door, Poole called after them.

"If you fail me, boy, or try any more of your devilish tricks, I'll kill you. You've been on borrowed time since I had you in my sights in that laboratory."

Ronin had the Dread Cloak driver drop them off several blocks from the safe house, and they walked the rest of the way. The sun was just coming up. Shops opened up as they passed by, and the sidewalks filled with people carrying coffee cups, on their way to work.

"It's there," Ronin said as they walked. "The augmenter gun is out there somewhere in the park. So is Dr. Hughes."

"How do you know?" Ben asked.

"Class Threes. Poole's enemy can actuate Class Threes. Poole can't. He needs the augmenter gun because he's expecting a showdown. And as paranoid as he is, there's no way he'd leave that gun in the city when his control over the gang is slipping. He'll have it somewhere close by."

Ben thought back to the park. It was big. Buildings everywhere. Probably Dread Cloaks everywhere, too. "So how do we find her?"

Ronin jammed his hands into his pockets. "Not sure yet. Let's get back to the crew and fill them in. We'll go from there. But there was some good news in all of that."

"What?"

"Poole doesn't think the gun is working yet. If he did, he wouldn't need us."

They made it back to the safe house, and Ronin let them in like he'd done the first time. But now Ben knew the way. Downstairs, the crew greeted them with relief and congratulations.

"You did good, kid!" Lykos held an ice pack to his jaw where Polly had punched him. "You're a natural."

"We were wrong to doubt you," Meg said.

Polly came up and put one cement pipe of an arm around Ben's shoulders. "You okay?"

"I'm fine," Ben said.

Polly nodded.

Ronin cleared his throat. "I'm fine, too, by the way."

Argus waved him off. "You're always fine, Ronin. More lives than Schrodinger's cat."

They didn't know how close it had been. They'd left before Ronin got back. They hadn't seen him almost get executed by Poole and his men. Ben wanted to say something about it, but Ronin nodded his head and spoke first.

"I told you," he said. "The plan was good. I know Poole."

But that wasn't true. Ronin had miscalculated Poole. Ben guessed he didn't want the crew to know that. Maybe he was afraid they'd lose confidence in the job.

"So." Ronin clapped his hands. "Coffee. Then on to the next phase."

Ben and Ronin spent the next few minutes filling the crew in on what they'd learned. Ronin went to the large table, pulled a map of the city from the stack of papers, and stuck it to the whiteboard with magnets.

"This is Mercer Beach." Ronin drew a circle on the map. "The augmenter gun is here, somewhere."

"I remember that place," Argus said. "Used to go there as a kid."

"Yeah, well. The clowns and magicians are gone now." Ronin stopped. He looked at the crew, and they all chuckled. "Like I was saying, the clowns are gone now. It's crawling with Dread Cloaks. The gun could be anywhere."

"So how do we find it?" Lykos asked.

"Our inside man," Argus said. "Ben just has to find the building that's most heavily guarded. That's where they'll be. Pretty straightforward."

"This isn't business as usual," Ronin said. "This isn't just another job. We'll have two packages we need to get out of there in one piece. The augmenter *and* the professor."

"Why the professor?" Argus asked. "Can't we leave her?"

Ben felt his shoulders tensing. For the crew, the only prize was the augmenter gun.

"The professor is part of the job," Ronin said.

"That makes no sense," Lykos said. "Wouldn't it be a lot simpler if we didn't bother with her?"

They could not leave Dr. Hughes behind. But Ronin would have a hard time explaining why to his crew. This was up to Ben.

"She's important to me," Ben said. "She taught me how to actuate. If you want me to be your inside man, she's part of the job."

The crew frowned and shook their heads. But that seemed to settle it.

"Will Poole have the professor and the gun together?" Meg asked.

"High probability," Ronin said. "He'll have her working on it."

"Then smash and grab." Argus punched his palm. "Ben finds out where they've got them, then we bust in and get them out."

"No," Ronin said. "They're too dug in out there, guarded by Poole's best. Too many." He studied the map. "We need to flush them out somehow. We stand the best chance if we can catch them on the move."

But what would make Poole move Dr. Hughes to a new location? He'd have to think it wasn't safe to keep her where she was anymore. He'd have to feel compromised or threatened.

"The raid," Ben said. "We use the raid to force Poole to move her."

"What raid?" Meg asked.

Ronin pointed his marker at Ben. "That's perfect, kid."

"What raid?" Meg asked again.

"The League raid," Ronin said.

"There's going to be a League raid?" Lykos asked.

"Not yet," Ben said. "But I'm going to make one."

CHAPTER
18

THE next day, Ronin drove Ben back to the Quantum League headquarters. The thought of it made Ben uncomfortable. Nervous. Sasha and Peter may have been comfortable there, but the League wasn't Ben's home any more than the Paracelsus crew safe house had been. Still, he was looking forward to seeing his friends again.

"Good luck in there," Ronin said.

"Thanks." It came out sounding more sarcastic than Ben had meant it.

"Hey, don't worry. The plan is good."

Ben rolled his eyes. "That's what you said about the last one."

"*This* plan is good," Ronin said. "Stick to the plan, and when you can't, you're pretty good at improvising."

Only this time, a made-up League raid wouldn't save him. Ben saw the building's steeple up ahead, and the butterflies in his stomach grew teeth.

"But another thing occurred to me this morning," Ronin said. "If you can get ahold of one, I'd like to see the schematics for the League's prison cells."

"Why?"

"Well . . ." Ronin adjusted his rearview mirror. "Look, I don't want you to worry about this, okay? But Poole is powerful. If things go south, we might need a place to put him. Can you do that? They'll have hard copies somewhere."

"I'll try."

"Good. And remember. This will only work if we keep it quiet. If Weathersky figures out what we're doing, he's gonna want in on it. He'll send agents, and the whole thing will blow up in our faces. Your Dr. Hughes will be as good as dead."

They pulled into the parking lot behind the church. "Got it," Ben said. He climbed out of the car.

Ronin leaned toward him over the passenger seat. "You can do this, kid."

"I know I can," Ben said, even though he wasn't sure.

"I'll come back tomorrow and check in."

Ben shut the door, and Ronin sped away. Ben turned toward the church's back door as it opened. Agent Spear and Agent Taggart came outside to greet him, followed by Peter and Sasha. Behind them came Mr. Weathersky. Peter took a deep breath and waved.

"Welcome back," Agent Spear said. He shook Ben's hand.

"Thank you," Ben said. He turned to Peter. "Hey."

"Hi," Peter said.

Sasha beamed. "Good to see you, Locus Boy."

"Good to see you, too."

"I'm relieved to have you back," Mr. Weathersky said. "But formalities must come before further pleasantries. We'll debrief in the library." He did a military turnabout and marched back inside.

Agent Spear motioned Ben toward the door. "After you, son."

Ben looked over his shoulder at Peter and Sasha. "See you guys later, I guess."

They nodded, and Ben went inside.

Ben spent the next half hour telling the story he and the Paracelsus crew had come up with. It was pretty close to the truth, with a few key omissions. He told how he and Ronin had gotten Poole's attention by breaking into his art collection. How they'd convinced Poole that Ben would spy on the League for him, making him a double agent. He left out the involvement of the other members of Ronin's crew, and the actual location of Poole's hideout.

"Where is Ronin now?" Agent Taggart asked.

"With Poole. He had to stay to maintain our cover."

"Have you learned anything about the portable augmenter's whereabouts?" Mr. Weathersky asked.

"Not yet," Ben said. "But he mentioned it when he recognized me."

"Was that a problem?" Agent Taggart asked. "Him recognizing you?"

"No," Ben said.

"Does he have it working yet?"

"No."

"How do you know?" Agent Spear asked.

"Right now, he's worried about a rival in his gang. There's somebody pretty powerful threatening his leadership. He wants the augmenter gun to take the guy out."

"Why would he need the augmenter for that?" Agent Spear asked. "Poole is a powerful Actuator."

"This rival can supposedly pull off Class Threes."

That got Agent Spear and Agent Taggart looking hard at each other across the table, as if thoughts were going back and forth through the air between them.

"Who could that be?" Agent Taggart finally asked. "There's no Class Three Actuator in the Dread Cloaks."

"There isn't a Class Three in the city right now." Agent Spear looked at Mr. Weathersky. "At least, not usually."

Something about what they were saying unsettled Ben. It felt familiar, like an itch that just kept coming back. It seemed like everywhere he looked, there was a mystery figure standing just out of view. Dr. Hughes had . . . Richter.

Poole had this powerful rival. And now that Ben thought about it, there was that extra member on Ronin's crew when they nabbed them during the jewel heist. None of them had ever talked about that guy. Why? Who was it? Who was Poole's rival? Who was Richter?

"So is this rival somebody we've missed?" Agent Taggart asked. "Or a new player in town?"

"Or is he simply the exaggeration of a gang lord?" Mr. Weathersky asked. "That seems likely to me. You were saying, Ben?"

"Well . . ." Ben put his other line of thought aside. *Stick to the plan*. "That's why Poole needs the augmenter gun. I think if it were working, he would have used it by now."

Mr. Weathersky nodded. "I think you are right. So long as he hasn't used it, I believe we can trust that Dr. Hughes is alive."

"So now that Ben's in place," Agent Spear said, "what should be our next move? We're running out of time."

"I need to take something back with me," Ben said. "Some kind of intel. I need to show Poole he can trust me." So far, the plan was going just as Ronin had said it would. Next, they would ask what kind of intel Poole would be expecting.

"All right," Agent Spear said. "Is there something specific that Poole's asking you to deliver?"

Ben almost smiled. "He asked me a lot about raids by League agents."

"Of course," Agent Taggart said. "He's worried we're going to come after the portable augmenter."

"That's exactly why he's asking," Ben said. "So I was thinking, and Ronin agrees, what if I bring him information on a raid? Something big, lots of agents, but in the future, far enough off this will all be over by then."

"So it doesn't have to be an actual raid," Agent Spear said.

Ben nodded. "Right."

Agent Spear turned to Mr. Weathersky. "We could draft a false order. With your signature of authorization. That should impress Poole."

"Perhaps," Mr. Weathersky said. "Before we commit to such a course of action, is there anything else you can tell us, Ben? Anything you're leaving out?"

"No, sir."

The air stirred. A feeling of . . . *trust* washed over Ben.

"Are you certain?" Mr. Weathersky asked. "If there is anything else, now is the time to tell us. You know you can trust us."

Ben looked at the director, the Old One, and he knew what was happening because he had figured out how to do it to Poole. He reached into his pocket, wrapped his hand around his Locus, and sent out waves of his own. *No.* You *can trust* me.

"There's nothing else to report at this time, sir," Ben said.

Agent Spear and Agent Taggart nodded, apparently satisfied.

But Mr. Weathersky stared at him. "Could I have a moment alone with Ben, please?"

Ben froze. He wondered if he'd just made a mistake, doing that. Why else would Mr. Weathersky want him alone? Had he seen through Ben's lies?

"Of course, sir," Agent Taggart said. Both agents gathered their papers, got up from the table, and left the room.

After they'd shut the door, the director sighed. "In my line of work, opportunities to speak candidly seldom come along. I'm grateful when they do."

This was off the script. Ben was going to have to improvise, but for now, he decided to talk as little as possible. He'd done this with his mom countless times.

"To have done what you just did," Mr. Weathersky said, "presumably on your own, without training is . . . unheard of."

Ben said nothing.

"You are an exceedingly rare kind of Actuator. A master of masters. One who understands people. And as you have no doubt observed, I am one as well. When did you first use your ability? Just now, that wasn't your first time. It was too clean."

Still Ben said nothing.

"Ben, I'm not sure what Dr. Hughes taught you about quantum mechanics, but imagine you've taken a single electron, loaded it into a gun, and fired it. As it moves, this electron is a *wave*, spread out, literally everywhere at once along its path."

Ben couldn't help it. "That makes no sense. It can't be everywhere at once."

"Oh, but it is. This has been *proven*. But you are not alone in your confusion. Even Einstein struggled with certain aspects of the quantum world." Mr. Weathersky traced his finger in a wavy pattern along the wood grain of the table. "This is called a *wave function* and the whole of it *is* the electron. That is, until you go to look for it along its path. Do you know what happens then?"

Say as little as possible. "No."

"You, the observer, *create* the electron's position as a particle. Right here." He pressed the tip of his index finger against the table. "Before you look, it is everywhere, but once you observe it, the electron is in a definite place. They call this a *collapse* of the wave. Do you know why I'm telling you this?"

"No."

"I've looked into your past. All the moves. The schools. Here, there, never settling. A mother you haven't ever been able to rely on."

Anger flared, white-hot, barely contained. "Don't you dare talk about my mom."

"Ben, what I'm telling you is this. In the wave function of your life, you must be your own observer. You must look, and find yourself."

Ben didn't know what to say. Or how to improvise. This was so far off the script, he almost didn't know what the job was anymore.

"Did you know," Mr. Weathersky said, "that an Actuator with an understanding of the human body could look at your X-ray and then stop your heart?" He pointed at Ben's chest. "Or burst a vein in your head? And that would be a small thing. A Class One."

That was something Ben had never even thought about. "I — I didn't —"

"Did you know that an Actuator with an understanding of molecular bonds in metal could weaken the welds holding a building together? A few well-placed cracks could bring down a skyscraper. Again, Class One."

Ben's throat dried up. He tried swallowing, but couldn't.

"Do you know what else is Class One?"

Ben shook his head.

"Tripping the detonator in a nuclear bomb."

This was all too much. Why was Mr. Weathersky telling him this? Was he trying to scare him? Was he threatening him?

The director rose from his chair. "There are evil people in the world, Ben. Evil people can do great harm with very little power. The Quantum League stands against such people. We are not perfect, but we are all the world has. Give that some thought as you go looking for yourself." He left Ben sitting at the table and went to the door. "I'll draft the false order for a raid on Poole. You'll take it back to him in the morning."

Then Mr. Weathersky was gone, and Ben was all alone.

• • •

Ben found Peter and Sasha in the dining room eating lunch. When they saw him walk in, they waved him over. He trudged to their table and collapsed into one of the chairs.

"Do you want to go get some food?" Peter asked.

Ben shook his head. "Not hungry."

"Okay," Sasha said. "Then talk. Tell us. What have you been doing?"

Ben shook his head again. "I'm not supposed to."

"But you're in?" Sasha asked. "You're in with the Dread Cloaks?"

"Yes."

"I have to say." Sasha looked over her shoulder. "After everything that everyone says about him, I had my doubts about Ronin."

"He just wants what I want," Ben said.

"What's that?" Peter asked.

"A piece of his life back."

Sasha and Peter both went quiet after that, and suddenly the food on their plates seemed more interesting to them than Ben. He thought about leaving it that way. Just letting the silence grow. But he couldn't. He couldn't understand why they didn't understand him. Why they didn't feel the same way.

"I went and saw my mom again," Ben said.

Sasha put down her fork, straightened her neck, and took a long and measured breath.

"Why would you keep doing that to yourself?" Peter asked.

Ben had wanted sympathy from them. He'd wanted understanding. "Don't you guys miss them?" he asked.

"Of course," Peter said. "But this is where I belong. This is where they accept me."

"What about you, Sasha?" Ben asked. "Do you miss them?"

The last time a question about Sasha's detachment had come up, she'd gotten pretty upset. But Ben was angry, and he didn't care if he upset her. She *should* be upset about it. Ben thought people should be more upset about a lot of things in the League, and if they were, maybe things would be different.

Sasha took a long drink of water from her cup. "Look, Ben. I really don't want to talk about this, okay?"

"Why?" Ben asked.

"I just don't. You . . . you can't change the past."

"No one's talking about the past," Ben said. "I'm asking if you miss them right now."

Sasha looked down at her lap.

"Do you?" Ben asked.

"Come on, Ben," Peter said. "That's enough."

But it didn't feel like enough. "Can't you even admit it to yourself?"

Sasha looked up at him. She wasn't mad like he was expecting. She was crying. He had hurt her. "To myself, all the time. Never to anyone else."

Suddenly, all the anger that had propped him up fell away, and Ben's resolve collapsed under his shame. "Sasha, I'm —"

She shook her head. "Don't. Just don't." She got up, threw her napkin on the table, and walked out of the dining room holding a hand over her mouth.

Ben fell forward, elbows on the table, covering his face with both hands. Why had he done that? Why was he taking out his anger and frustration on his friends?

"She's been really worried about you," Peter said.

That only made Ben feel worse.

CHAPTER
19

LATER that night, as Ben lay in bed, the echoes of what he'd said to Sasha sounded over and over in his head. He stared at the ceiling, thinking about her tears, and how she'd looked walking away from the table. He would apologize in the morning, before he went back to Poole.

"I'm up to Class Two actuations," Peter said.

Ben looked over. His friend was awake, too. "That's awesome."

"Sasha helped me. We've been training a lot the past couple of days."

"Good. I'm glad."

"The thing is —" Peter paused, and in the dark, his hesitation seemed longer than it probably was. "If they told me I could go back tomorrow, I wouldn't. If they offered to reattach me, I'd say no."

Ben rolled to face him. "Are you serious?"

Peter stayed on his back, looking up. "I'm serious. So I guess what I'm saying is, if you're doing this for me at all, don't. But do what you have to do for yourself. I'm behind you on that."

Ben had thought about this before, wondered if leaving the League would mean leaving Peter behind. Ben didn't like that thought, but it was Peter's choice. "Thanks for having my back," he said.

"Sasha has your back, too. You should know that."

"Thanks." The guilt about what he'd said to her returned. "Has she ever talked to *you* about her family? What her life was like before she came to the League?"

"No."

"I wonder why she won't talk about it."

Peter yawned. "Just . . . just let it go." He was silent after that, and snoring not long after.

With everyone asleep, it was time for Ben to execute a new part of the job. Ronin wanted plans for the League's prison cells to hold Poole, if needed. Ben didn't know where to find those, but he knew where to look. He climbed out of bed, grabbed his boots, and slipped across the room in his socks. He looked back to see if anyone had woken up or noticed him, and it didn't seem like they had. So he went up the stairs.

The building hallways were still lit, even though every-one had gone home. Ben pulled on his boots and laced them up. He knew agents patrolled the building at night, keeping watch. He hoped he wouldn't bump into one of them, but if he did, it wouldn't be a big deal. He was a recruit. He belonged there. Maybe he had insomnia, and maybe a walk or some fresh air helped him get to sleep.

Ben turned in the direction of a room he knew about, but had never been inside before. It was the file room where they kept all the dossiers and League records, and if there were schematics for the prison cells anywhere in the building, that's where they'd be.

He made it there without running into anyone, and peeked around the corner. The hallway was empty. He scur-ried to the door and tried the handle, even though he expected it to be locked. It was. But he'd seen Polly do this, so he thought maybe he could, too.

He listened for the sounds of anyone approaching, and got down on his knees. Like the others in the building, it was an old-fashioned lock. He focused on the cylinder where the key slid in, its shape, and with his Locus in hand, he tried a simple actuation to rotate it.

It jiggled, but something stopped it, like Ben had inserted the wrong key.

He didn't have any idea what the inside of the lock looked like. He hadn't studied them the way Polly had, so he couldn't visualize which parts to move.

He heard distant footsteps.

They seemed to be getting louder. Coming toward him.

Ben suppressed the panic that rose with each footfall. He couldn't actuate if he panicked. He turned his attention back to the lock. He thought he could probably force it, with a strong enough actuation. But he worried the guard would be able sense it, and besides, then the lock would be broken and the League would know someone had been in the file room.

The footsteps were pretty close now. In the next hallway. Ben had seconds, tops.

He remembered a time when he'd accidentally locked himself and his mom out of the bathroom, and he had to go, bad. His mom had slipped a credit card into the crack by the handle and pushed that metal sliding bar in, opening the door.

Ben didn't have a credit card. But this door had one of those metal sliding bars, like the other doors in the building. He tried to remember what they looked like, felt like, then closed his eyes to visualize this one. Ben felt the shape and the size of the metal in his mind as if with his fingers.

The footsteps were just around the corner. It was hard to ignore them and concentrate, but Ben held his Locus and actuated a motion that pushed the bar in.

The door popped open.

Ben flew inside the room and closed the door behind him. Then he held his breath and listened.

The footsteps sounded like they were in the hallway now. They came closer, right up to the door, and kept going.

Ben let out his breath and turned to face the room. Rows of filing cabinets stood in formation from one wall to the other. A desk near the door to Ben's left bore a lamp. He switched it on, hoping it wasn't bright enough to attract attention if the guard walked by again, and started down the aisles.

The labels on the cabinets didn't make any sense. Just numbers and letters and periods. But Ben figured schematics would be pretty big, so he went to the filing cabinet with wide, flat drawers and started digging through them. The first few drawers were full of maps: road maps, topographical maps, even what looked like a map of the city's sewer system. The next drawers had blueprints for all kinds of structures. Then Ben opened a drawer that seemed closer to what he was after, with technical diagrams and designs with complicated labels like, *Interferometer Arrangement for Two Mirrors in Quantum Superposition*. Ben plowed through the rest of them, scanning as fast as he could, until he found what Ronin wanted.

Actuation Suppression Cell.

He smiled to himself and whipped the plans out of the drawer. To hide them, he rolled them up tight and stuck them down his pant leg, then headed for the door. On his way there, one of the cabinets caught his eye. It had an actual label.

AGENTS: PROSPECTIVE

He wondered if Sasha would be in there, but only doubted for a moment whether he should look. He opened the drawer and flipped along the tabbed files to the L's until he came to LAMBERT, SASHA. He pulled her file and opened it up.

There was her picture, the same black hair, but instead of a blue streak, she had a red one. Beneath that he found her basic information: EYE COLOR. HEIGHT. WEIGHT. But many of the other lines had been left blank. No place of birth. No names of parents. Not even a date of birth. In the space marked DETACHMENT DATE, someone had written in: *PENDING*.

Ben was stunned. According to this, Sasha had never been detached. She had lied to them. But why had the League left her attached? And why did she get so upset whenever Ben brought it up? She had nothing to be upset about. She could still go home.

Ben heard footsteps out in the hallway, the guard returning. He shoved the file back in the drawer, leaped to the desk, and managed to kill the lamp just before the footsteps passed in front of the door.

Several moments of silence passed before Ben opened the door, just a crack, and peered out. No one there, and no one coming that he could hear. He made sure the door was relocked, and then slipped out into the hallway. Minutes later, he was in bed.

But thoughts of Sasha still kept him awake, and the next

morning, he sought her out. He wanted to talk to her before Ronin returned and they left again.

He found her eating breakfast in the dining room, and grabbed the seat next to her.

"You weren't ever detached," he whispered.

Her back stiffened. "What? How did you —?"

"That's not important. I just want to know why you lied to me. And if you're not detached, why are you still here?"

Sasha set her spoon down slowly, staring at it, like it might try to escape her hand. "Look. This *really* isn't any of your business."

"I thought we were friends." Ben had to clear his throat. "You know what this means to me."

"We *are* friends." Sasha looked at him for several moments, and then leaned closer. "Of course we're friends. I'm sorry, it's not that I ever meant to lie to you. . . . Look, there are other kinds of detachment, okay? It doesn't have to be quantum to be real."

"What do you mean? Other kinds, like what?"

"Like —"

"Ready, kid?" Ronin walked into the room, flanked by Agent Spear and Agent Taggart.

Sasha leaned back and looked away as Ronin took a seat next to Ben, across from her.

"I've already eaten," Ronin said. "The food is better than I remember. But still not great. You want something before we go?"

Ben shook his head.

Sasha gave him a darting smile and rose from her chair. "Be safe, okay? We'll talk more when you get back." She left the room.

Ben looked at Agent Spear. "Have you seen Peter?"

"Not this morning," Agent Spear said.

"Do I have time to go find him and say good-bye?" Ben asked.

"I'm afraid not," Agent Taggart said. "Mr. Weathersky wants you both back with Poole as soon as possible."

Ben nodded.

Agent Spear put an envelope on the table. "There you go. Mr. Weathersky signed it this morning."

Ronin looked down. "What's this?"

"False orders for a League raid," Agent Taggart said. "Something to build Poole's confidence in Ben."

Ronin nodded and stood. "Perfect. Let's go, kid. I don't like being here any longer than I have to be." He looked at Agent Spear and Agent Taggart. "Some offense intended."

Ben picked up the envelope. "Did Mr. Weathersky say anything else?"

"Good luck," Agent Spear said. "And good work. That goes for me, too, son."

"Thanks," Ben said.

He followed Ronin out back to his car, and they drove away without any of the send-off they'd been given the last time. Ben left the League headquarters feeling like he'd disappointed and hurt the people there he cared about.

"You okay?" Ronin asked.

"Yeah," Ben said. He reached down his pants.

"Whoa," Ronin said. "What are you —?"

Ben pulled out the rolled-up plans. "Here. The actuation suppression cell."

"You did it?" Ronin took the plans, tapped the dash with them, and then tossed them into the backseat. "I'm impressed, kid."

Ben opened up the envelope and read the raid order. It was perfect. "We just have to change the date on this, and we're all set."

Ronin drove them to a twenty-four-hour copy center. They bought some time on a computer and scanned in the raid order. From there, it was a pretty simple thing to erase the old date, and put in a new one, two days away. Then they erased Mr. Weathersky's signature, and printed a brand-new raid order.

"You're up, kid," Ronin said.

Ben took the original order, with the signature, and laid it side by side with the new order. He'd done the same thing with his mom's signature, but that had also taken a lot of practice. He grabbed a pen and some scratch paper. He filled up two sheets before he thought it looked passable. Ronin agreed, so Ben tried on the new order.

He sat back, eyes jumping back and forth between the real signature and his forgery. It looked good.

"I think you got it on the first try," Ronin said.

"Yeah?"

"Looks good to me. Let's go with it."

They shredded everything but the new order, and got back in the car. Ronin drove them out to Mercer Beach the same way Poole had brought them. In the daylight, the abandoned neighborhoods and strip malls around the refinery looked even worse.

"Which house are we going to use?" Ben asked.

"Not sure yet," Ronin said. "But the plan is the same. Poole will bring Hughes in a convoy right through here. Argus will give us some cover. Lykos and Meg will create a distraction with Polly, while you and I strike from the inside and get Hughes and the augmenter out of there."

"Right."

"After I drop you off, I'm going to meet up with the rest of the crew to finalize details of the ambush."

"You're not coming with me?"

"No."

Ben ran his thumb along the edge of the envelope. He didn't like the thought of going back to Poole alone.

"You'll be all right, kid. The time to worry about a paranoid man is when you confront his fears, not when you confirm them. Just remember why you're doing this."

Ben didn't need to remember. His reasons clung to the back of everything he had done so far, and everything he was about to do. He stayed silent for the rest of the ride, and Ronin dropped him off at the edge of the parking lot.

Ben walked across the wide expanse of broken pavement. Flaking paint still hung on in places where the parking stalls had been, but weeds and grass now worked to claim them. A breeze ripe with refinery stench wrinkled his nose. It took several minutes for Ben to reach the amusement park's entrance. As he approached, a couple of Dread Cloaks appeared from inside the old ticket booths.

Time to fake it. He went for demanding. "I'm Ben, the League recruit. Where's Poole?"

That seemed to catch the men off guard. They hesitated, and Ben forced his way into the gap.

"Never mind, I know where his office is." He strode right between them. They didn't try to stop him.

Ben entered Mercer Beach and saw it for the first time in daylight, and from the front. Even if it hadn't been run-down, Ben could see the place was old. The style of the buildings, the decorations, the paint jobs. It looked like it belonged in the kind of movies his mom watched, where the actors wore white pants and bow ties and regularly broke into big song-and-dance numbers.

He plodded down an old boardwalk, the wood planks splitting and loose at the ends. It followed the edge of a wide promenade, and to his right, another boardwalk ran parallel along the far side. Between them, the dirt was as hard-packed as cement, and rusted gates and fences marked the empty places where rides used to be. To his left, a succession of booths, stripped of everything but the paint, still advertised games, cotton candy, popcorn, and corn dogs.

He passed a few buildings, and wondered if Poole had Dr. Hughes in one of them. The House of Mirrors? The Hall of Curiosities and Wonders? Then he came to the carousel, with its candy-cane paint and silent, stampeding horses in every possible color. He could almost hear the strains of the frantic organ music coming out of it, the screams and laughter as it spun around.

A boot scuffed behind him. Ben turned to see about a dozen Dread Cloaks spread out between the boardwalks. They stood back a short distance, just following him, watching him.

He moved on, trying to keep his pace steady. Ahead of him rose the arena, and the Ferris wheel towered high above that. When he reached Poole's building, several Dread Cloaks met him at the front entrance.

Ben aimed for the space between them. "I need to see Poole."

But they put out their arms and blocked his way.

"Hold still," one of them said. It was the redhead from Poole's office.

"What's going —?"

One of the other Dread Cloaks came up and grabbed Ben from behind.

The redhead smirked. "We gotta search you. Nobody sees Poole without getting searched first."

Ben ran down everything he had on him, and didn't think there would be a problem. "Fine."

The Dread Cloak's eyes narrowed. "I'm Riggs. You don't recognize me. I was wearing a mask. But you almost did me in with a bolt of lightning."

So that's it. This was the guy Ben had knocked out during the attack on the lab. That explained why he'd been so hostile. Ben was a bit more worried now.

Riggs felt up and down his arms and legs, around his torso. "Pockets."

Ben reached in, pulled out the two things he carried. The raid order, and his Locus. Riggs took both, and looked at the envelope first.

"That's what Poole is expecting right now," Ben said.

"And this?" Riggs rolled the Locus around in his hand.

"That's nothing," Ben said. He didn't think it would be a good idea to let on what that piece of stone meant to him.

"Kinda weird, carrying around a fossil."

"I'm weird," Ben said, but his voice sounded stiff.

Riggs looked into Ben's eyes, then at the stone. "You think I don't know a Locus when I see one?"

"Give it back," Ben said.

Riggs handed him the envelope. "Poole will see you now."

Ben needed his Locus. The job depended on him actuating with the crew. He started trembling, but kept it out of his voice. "Give me the stone."

Riggs took a step backward. "You Class One or Class Two with this?"

Ben didn't answer.

Riggs shouted. "Class One or Class Two?"

Ben clenched his jaw. "Class Two."

Riggs nodded. Then he set the Locus on the ground.

What was he doing?

The Dread Cloak holding Ben tightened his grip as Riggs stuck out one of his hands and flexed his fingers. Ben felt an actuation stirring.

"No!" Ben fought to break free. "Don't —"

Riggs flicked his hand. Ben's Locus shot off the ground, straight at the arena, where it shattered against the wall, leaving a little impact crater behind. Ben almost cried out. The Dread Cloak behind him let him go.

"What Class are you now?" Riggs asked.

Ben just stared at him.

"Go on in." He and the other Dread Cloaks stepped aside. "Poole's waiting."

CHAPTER
20

BEN sat before Poole in one of the armchairs, completely powerless. They were up in Poole's office above the arena, and Poole leaned forward on his desk, looking down at the raid order resting between his hands. Ben focused on staying calm and hoped Ronin was right about paranoid men, because without his Locus, he was just an Ennay. An Imp. If Poole turned on him, Ben was defenseless.

"How did you come by this?" Poole asked.

"I told you," Ben said. "I'm a prodigy. The League trusts me. It wasn't hard to steal."

Poole sat down. "This is Weathersky's signature."

Ben nodded. "He's in town to personally oversee the operation."

"This is two days away."

"That's right."

"You told me a week."

"Weathersky moved it up." So far, they were on script, Locus or not. "They're worried about Dr. Hughes and the portable augmenter."

Poole snapped a glare at Ben. "I know you've put it together, you and Ronin. You know why I'm out here, hiding like a rat."

"And we figure the augmenter's probably out here, too." Ben shrugged. "So?"

"So?" Poole took the raid order and folded it into precise thirds, creasing it with his thumbnail against the desk. "Do you expect me to believe you have no interest in it?"

"I've used it. I don't see the big deal. You can probably do more damage to the League with it than I could."

"I doubt Ronin thinks the same way you do."

Ben chuckled. "Ronin doesn't even think it works. He says portable augmentation is impossible, and you're a desperate man clinging to your last hope."

Poole's eyebrows lifted. "Ronin said that, did he?"

Ben nodded.

"Where is Ronin now?"

"I don't know," Ben said. "I told you, I was never his man."

Poole slipped the raid order into a pocket inside his vest. He sat back, closed his eyes, and rubbed the tip of his index finger back and forth across his forehead. "Two days."

"Can't you make a stand here?" Ben asked. "Just use the augmenter."

Poole shook his head. "That worthless Imp hasn't got it working yet. I've tried it. Many times."

"What if you just pull all the Dread Cloaks out here from the city? Build up an army."

"I dare not trust any of them. The upstart might use the opportunity to send in spies and saboteurs." He suddenly slammed the desk with his fist, and Ben flinched. "Two days! That's not enough time!"

"I'm sure you —"

He jumped to his feet. "This was supposed to be my hour of victory! My defeat of the League!"

"You can still —"

"Shut up, you whelp! You cur! You know-nothing!"

Ben snapped his mouth closed. He realized he had started to confront Poole's fears by reassuring him. He needed to switch tactics, play it how Ronin had said to work a paranoid man. *Confirm* Poole's fears.

"Look," Ben said. "The League is coming for you. Here. And they're coming hard. They're not taking any chances with the augmenter."

"Then we need to make sure it isn't here for them to find, don't we?"

"You're going to move it?"

"Yes. If I start making the arrangements now, we can do it tomorrow night." He pulled out his phone.

"What do you want me to do?" Ben asked.

"You?" Poole started dialing. "You're going to sit right there. No devilish tricks. I'm not letting you out of my sight."

So far, things had all gone the way Ronin and his crew had planned. Except for one thing. Riggs had destroyed Ben's Locus, and he didn't know what that would mean for the ambush tomorrow night.

Poole meant what he said. The rest of that day, Ben sat in his office as the gang lord organized the transfer. First, Poole had to pick a new location, so he made calls. Dread Cloaks came and went, and Poole waited. By that afternoon, Poole had chosen a place, but then he had to double- and triple-check it. Ben tried to listen in and figure out where it was, but couldn't get anything specific.

The next phase, Poole called in specific Dread Cloaks by name, the ones Ben guessed he still trusted. Poole sent them ahead to secure the location. Then it was more waiting. Ben paced around the office, and looked through the windows down at the stage. He even tried some of the buttons and switches on the control panel to see what they did.

"Don't touch that," Poole said.

By evening, Ben was more bored than nervous. Apparently, being paranoid took a lot of work and energy. Would Poole keep at it through the whole night?

Ben grew hungry. Tired. It was getting late. He had

slumped down pretty far in the armchair, his eyelids heavy, when there was yet another knock at the office door.

"Ah, supper." Poole accepted a pizza box from one of his Dread Cloaks. He handed it to Ben. "This is the favorite food of every child in the country, is it not?"

Ben sat up. "Sure. I guess."

The pizza was a little cold, but Ben didn't care. He ate slice after slice, more than half the pie. Then, with a full stomach, he slumped back into the armchair and closed his eyes.

He woke to Poole's voice. Ben bolted upright, a massive kink in his neck. It was morning.

"Yes!" Poole said into his phone. "Three vehicles. We can't attract too much attention. But I want every man capable of Class Two actuations. No exceptions." His sunken eyes looked even darker around the edges than usual. Ben guessed he hadn't slept at all. "And find Ronin!" He hung up the phone and glanced at Ben. "Ah, you're awake. Are you hungry for breakfast?"

Ben yawned. "Sure."

Poole pointed at the pizza box. "Then finish that."

"Okay." Ben didn't mind cold pizza. He lifted the lid and grabbed a stiff slice. "So where are we at?"

"*We* are nowhere. You are sitting there today while I make final arrangements for the transfer tonight." He stopped what he was doing. "Unless you have some idea where Ronin is."

"No idea. But I'm sure he'll turn up." *And it had better be soon.* They had to come up with a new plan, something that didn't require Ben to actuate.

But the hours passed, and Ronin never showed.

By that afternoon, Poole had become increasingly agitated. "Where *is* he? I should have killed him. I had him, and I should have killed him."

Ben acted as nonchalant as he could manage, but inside, he was panicking. He didn't know where Ronin was, or what had happened, but they were running out of time.

"I don't like this, I don't like this at all." Poole paced laps around his desk. "Ronin on the loose. Perhaps I need to reconsider."

"Reconsider what?" Ben asked.

"The transfer."

"Forget about Ronin," Ben said. "He doesn't even know you're moving the augmenter tonight. What about the Quantum Lea —?"

"Damn the League, the League, the League!" Poole pressed his palms against his temples, squeezing his own head like a vise. Then he relaxed. The man was coming loose. "You're right. You're right. Ronin means nothing. It's the raid."

"The raid," Ben said. *Keep him thinking about the raid. Confirm his fears.*

Things quieted down after that. Ben and Poole went downstairs, and everyone who would be involved that night gathered on the floor of the arena. By evening, Poole had made all the preparations, handpicked his men, checked every detail over and over and over again, and now they were just waiting for the order to move out.

That was when Poole's phone rang. He listened for a moment, and then he started screaming. "You listen to me! You're dead! You hear me? Dead! And after that, I'm going to take out the rest of your crew! You —" He pulled the phone away from his ear and stared at it. "He . . . hung up on me."

"Was that Ronin?" Ben asked.

"Yes." Poole put his phone away. "He has removed himself from the equation. The hour has come. Let's go."

"What do you mean?" Inside, Ben became frantic. That sounded like Ronin wasn't coming. But Ronin had to come. Ben couldn't do the job without him. "Where's Ronin?"

"The coward has run off."

"What about —?" Ben swallowed. "Did he say anything about me?"

"Yes. He said to tell you that you're on your own."

On his own? Ben had no idea what that meant. Was it now up to him alone to free Dr. Hughes during the ambush? Or had Ronin and his crew abandoned the job altogether, along with Ben?

Poole grabbed Ben by the neck. "Not to fear, devilish one. You were never his, remember?" He dragged Ben along with him, behind the stage and out the back door. They piled into three waiting SUVs. Poole shoved Ben into the middle car, and climbed in after him, leaving a space between them.

The vehicles pulled out and headed for the park exit, but along the way they stopped behind another building. Two Dread Cloaks emerged from a back door, and between them Ben saw Dr. Hughes. She looked frightened as they hauled her to the car. Poole got out, took Dr. Hughes by the arm, and pushed her into the vehicle with Ben.

He got in and shut the door. "Isn't this a pleasant reunion, the pupil and the student."

"Ben?" Her round eyes were red and watery.

"Hi, Dr. Hughes," Ben said. A Dread Cloak loaded a plastic crate into the back of the car, and Ben figured it had to be the augmenter gun.

Dr. Hughes shook her head. "What are you —?"

"And that's enough of that," Poole said. "Roll out!"

The SUVs pulled forward and followed the road to the park's back gate. From there, they charged across the parking lot. Ben didn't know what was about to happen, or what he was going to do, but he had Dr. Hughes beside him. He hadn't seen her since the Dread Cloaks had attacked her lab, and so much had happened since then. She looked tired, but she was alive, and she wasn't hurt, and he felt reassured by that. Now it was up to him to get them both out of there. Somehow.

The convoy reached the edge of the parking lot, and soon drove under the Mercer Beach sign. The night was clear, the streets completely deserted.

"It's good to see you," Dr. Hughes whispered.

Ben nodded, his attention on the road ahead. He looked for signs, anything at all, of the Paracelsus crew. But the strip malls gave way to houses, and pretty soon they would reach the freeway. If the crew didn't show, what could Ben do without his Locus? Without it, he was just an ordinary kid, trapped in a vehicle with a paranoid murderer. What would Poole do when the raid never happened, and he figured out what Ben had done?

Ben had to escape with Dr. Hughes. Soon. Now. They could hide among all these empty houses, just like the Paracelsus crew had planned to do. Could they make a jump for it from the moving car? That seemed too risky, and the Dread Cloaks would be on them in no time, actuations firing. No, he needed to think of something else. Without moving his head, his eyes roamed around the vehicle. Then he remembered the crate in back.

The portable augmenter. He didn't need a Locus. He just had to get his hands on that gun. But how?

"Fog, sir," the SUV's driver said.

Ben looked ahead, hope flaring inside him, as they plowed into a bank of mist so thick they lost sight of the vehicle in front of them. *Argus.*

Poole looked across the seat at Ben. "Devilish tricks."

Ben just shook his head.

The first explosion flashed in front of them, blinding, deafening, and then a second ripped through the fog behind them. That was Meg and Lykos, taking out the other cars.

"AMBUSH!" Poole pounded on the driver's shoulder. "GO, GO!"

The driver slammed down on the gas, throwing Ben back against the seat. But the SUV didn't get far before it jolted and slowed.

"Our tires are out!" the driver shouted.

That was Polly, blowing their valves, and that was supposed to be Ben's cue. His and Ronin's. But Ronin wasn't there, and Ben didn't have his Locus. There was only one thing to do. He unbuckled and heaved himself over the seat into the back. Poole tried to grab him.

"What are you —?"

Ben kicked him away and flipped the lid off the crate. There was the gun. He grabbed it and aimed it at Poole. "Move and I'll shoot! Try to actuate and I'll shoot!"

Poole snickered. "It doesn't work, you stupid, stupid boy."

"It does for me." Ben went for ice, just like he had the first time he'd used it. It was easy, with all the water in the air from Argus's fog. The temperature inside the car plummeted. Poole's breath became visible in the cold, and Ben sensed the force of his own actuation. "Can you feel that, Poole?"

Poole's cheeks reddened. His whole face quivered with rage around his wide, bloodshot eyes.

"Dr. Hughes," Ben said, "get out of the car. Don't be afraid of the big guy."

Dr. Hughes sat there for a minute, and then did what Ben said, disappearing into the fog.

"The big guy?" Ben could almost see Poole's thoughts racing to the realization of how he'd been played. "The Paracelsus crew?"

Ben kept the gun trained on Poole, the actuation poised at the edge of reality, and reached behind him with his other hand. "It's easy to get someone to believe something they want to believe." He felt for the handle, popped it, and the back of the SUV lifted open with a whiny hiss.

"You're still on borrowed time," Poole said. "You and the Paracelsus crew."

"Actually," Ben climbed out onto the street, "once your rival hears about this, I think you're the one on borrowed time."

Poole's face blanched.

Ben turned and ran into the fog.

CHAPTER
21

BEN stumbled ahead, unsure of where he was going. He didn't think Poole would come after him, not if he thought the Paracelsus crew was out there somewhere in the fog. But Ben had to find the safe house and get off the streets before the air cleared.

"Polly!" he whispered. "Dr. Hughes! Argus!"

Suburban homes loomed out of the mist around him, looking even more haunted than they had before. Ben ran down uneven sidewalks that seemed to heave up under his feet, in and out of cul-de-sacs, over lawns left to dry up and die.

"Meg! Lykos!"

"Ben!"

He stopped and oriented toward the voice. That sounded like Argus, and not too far away. Ben cupped his hand to his mouth. "I'm here!"

"Ben, this way!"

Ben ran toward the voice, between two houses, through a backyard, and almost tripped over a child's abandoned tricycle. He came to a low picket fence, and climbed over it.

"You're almost here." Argus sounded very close now. "Hurry."

Ben ran another few yards, and the back of a house materialized. Argus stood on the cement patio, near an open sliding door.

"Come," he said.

"Dr. Hughes?"

"She's inside."

Ben slowed down and walked through the door. He froze as Argus slid the door shut behind him. In the middle of what was once a living room, Polly held Dr. Hughes by the arm, and she looked even more terrified of the giant than she had of Poole. Meg and Lykos held Ronin between them. He'd been beaten, both eyes blackened, a busted and swollen lip. His head lolled, and he seemed barely conscious.

Argus snatched the portable augmenter from Ben's hand. "I'll take that."

Ben spun around. "What's going on?"

"We're taking the gun," Argus said. "And we're going to sell it to the highest bidder."

"We?" What was Argus talking about? Ben shook his head. He looked again at Ronin and realized why he hadn't come. "But —"

"Ronin thought he could use you to cross us," Meg said. "But we knew from the moment he brought you to the safe house."

After everything Ben had done. Working the Paracelsus crew, working Poole. He had rescued Dr. Hughes, had the gun in his hand. They were so close. "How . . . ?"

"He didn't ask about the jewels." Lykos looked down at Ronin. "Not once. We'd just done a job, and he never even asked about his cut. We knew something was wrong."

Ben lost feeling in his arms and legs. He thought he might go down, but he refused. To these people, he was still the kid capable of anything. "So what now?"

"Now," Argus said, "we take the gun and we leave."

"What happens to us?" Ben asked.

"Well, Polly has insisted you go free," Argus said. "You and your professor. And the thing is, kid, we like you. So we're good. Bygones be bygones."

"And Ronin?" Ben asked.

"He played you," Meg said. "He played us, he played Poole, and he played the League."

"Worst thing we can do to him now is cut him loose," Lykos said. "Throw him to the wolves."

"There might be one more thing." Argus walked up to Ronin and reached inside his jacket pocket. He pulled out

Ronin's keys. "I think we'll take his car. Conveniently parked right outside."

"You —" Ronin lifted his head and tried speaking for the first time, his voice raspy and weak. "You've always wanted my car."

Argus slipped the keys into his pocket. "It'll look better on me anyway."

He nodded to Meg and Lykos, and they threw Ronin to the ground. He didn't even try to catch himself, and went down hard. Polly nudged Dr. Hughes toward Ben and handed her off.

"Take it easy, kid," the giant said.

The Paracelsus crew moved to the front door. Lykos and Meg went out first, and then Polly ducked through the door. Before Argus left, he turned back. "Word of advice, kid. Leave Ronin and clear out fast. It won't take Poole long to find this place." Then he was gone.

Ben dropped to his knees beside Ronin. "Are you okay? Get up, we gotta move."

Ronin shook his head. "Wait."

"Wait?" Ben said. "Wait for what?"

Another second passed, and then Ronin staggered to his feet. He straightened, both hands on his lower back, wincing, and then trudged toward the front door. Ben felt an actuation forming.

"Ronin, you can't go after them," Ben said. "They'll kill you."

Ronin smiled back at him, a confident glint in his eyes, and stepped outside.

Ben followed after him, and Dr. Hughes came behind. The fog had started lifting, and out in the driveway, the Paracelsus crew had climbed into Ronin's car. Argus sat in the driver's seat, Polly beside him, Meg and Lykos in the back. But they were just sitting there, looking around, confused. Ronin laughed and shambled over to Argus. He leaned his shoulder against the car and motioned with a twirl of his finger for Argus to roll the window down.

Argus did. "What did you do, Ronin?"

"A little upgrade." Ronin knocked on the roof. "Call it an antitheft device. My car is now equipped with the latest actuation suppression technology, courtesy of the Quantum League." He held up his hand. "And you've no doubt felt the actuation I have all warmed up. A little Class One, and this car blows sky-high."

Ben wanted to laugh. That was what Ronin had wanted with the plans. He had said they were for Poole, but really, they were for his own crew. Had he known they were going to double-cross him?

"Hand it over," Ronin said. "I will not ask twice."

Argus didn't look quite as angry as Poole had, but almost. He passed the augmenter gun through the open window.

Ronin took it and limped away from the car. "Be grateful I'm not the type to hold a grudge and treat you in kind."

He walked up to the house's garage door. "Help me with this, Ben?"

Ben didn't know what was going on, but he walked over and lifted open the garage door. Inside, he saw another car. Ronin opened the trunk and put the augmenter gun inside. Then he walked to the driver's side and unlocked it. "Get in, Ben. You, too, Dr. Hughes."

Once they were all inside, Ronin turned the key, and the car rumbled to life. He put it in reverse and inched out of the garage, right past the Paracelsus crew trapped in his old car. Ben couldn't resist, and he waved good-bye to them. Argus, Lykos, and Meg all glared at him, but Polly waved back.

"I'm going to miss that car," Ronin said as he reached the street. "But this'll do." He threw the car into first gear, and Ben heard the tires squeal as they launched down the road.

During the drive back to the city, Ben filled Ronin in on what had happened with Poole and the Dread Cloaks for the past two days, while Dr. Hughes had somehow fallen asleep in the backseat.

"When you didn't come back," Ben said, "I didn't know what I was going to do."

"Sorry, kid," Ronin said. "I had to let the crew think they'd gotten the jump on me. But I knew you could handle it. I've seen you actuate."

"But that's just it," Ben said. "I couldn't actuate. One of the Dread Cloaks destroyed my Locus."

"You use a Locus?" Ronin asked. "How did I not know that?"

Ben shrugged. "Never came up."

"So, wait." Ronin crinkled one eye at him. "You were in the car with Poole during the ambush, and you couldn't actuate?"

"Right," Ben said.

"What did you do?"

"I grabbed the augmenter gun."

"That thing works, huh?"

"It does for me."

The sun was just coming up as they approached the League headquarters, the tip of the steeple lit by a slice of golden light, while the rest of it lay in shadow. Ronin suddenly jerked the steering wheel and pulled them over to the side of the road. The jostling woke up Dr. Hughes.

Ben looked over at Ronin. "What —?"

"Get out of the car, kid."

Ben pointed up the road. "But it's just —"

The air stirred with an actuation. Ben froze. He didn't know what was happening.

"I'm not gonna kill you," Ronin said. "But I'll hurt you if I have to. Now get out of the car. You, too, Dr. Hughes."

Dr. Hughes hurried from the backseat onto the sidewalk.

Ben stayed where he was. "What are you doing?"

"I'm taking the portable augmenter. What else?"

"But . . ." Ben didn't know what to say. Ronin had coached him, taught him, saved him. Even if Ben had had his Locus, he was so confused right now, he wasn't sure he could actuate a thing.

"Look, kid. I could have left you back by the refinery. But I didn't. I didn't want to risk the chance of Poole finding you. You're safe now."

"Ronin, please —"

"GET OUT OF THE CAR!"

Ben flinched. He opened the door, hopped out, then turned to ask, "What about your daughter?"

Ronin laughed. "Mr. Weathersky doesn't have my daughter. Remember what I told you? The easiest way to play someone is to tell them what they want to hear. Anytime somebody is telling you what you want to hear, you'd better pay attention to what they're *really* saying."

"But . . ." Tears came to Ben's eyes. A sob caught in his throat. This was too much. This, of all things. "Ronin — my mom."

Ronin looked away, down the road. He cleared his throat. "Sorry, kid. Now shut the door."

Ben shut it.

Ronin sped away.

• • •

"This isn't your fault," Agent Spear said. "You hear me, son?"

Ben stared at the agent. They were sitting in the library with Agent Taggart, Dr. Hughes, and Mr. Weathersky. The director had filled Dr. Hughes in on the League and its mission, and she'd seemed a lot less shocked by it than Ben would have thought. But then, she'd already been kidnapped by a gang of Actuators, so a self-appointed police force of Actuators probably made perfect sense.

Then it was Ben's turn. He told them everything he had done, even the part about stealing the plans for the prison cells. But to make his report without breaking down, he'd had to empty himself of all thoughts, all feelings. Like a damaged jet fighter dropping its missiles harmlessly before it crashed. Fewer casualties that way.

"You're right," Mr. Weathersky said. "It isn't Ben's fault. I'm the one who trusted Morrow. I authorized the mission."

But it wasn't the director's fault. Ben had helped Ronin do things the League had known nothing about. Ben had lied, because he'd been angry with the League, and now he was paying the price. It was Ben's fault, too.

"Ben," Mr. Weathersky said. "Whatever it is you're thinking, I want you to stop. You couldn't have known. You did what you thought was best."

"I should have —"

"Stop," Mr. Weathersky said. "There is no point to it. There is no actuation for changing the past."

"That's right," Agent Taggart said. "We just need to go after Morrow."

"But what about my mom?" Ben asked. It didn't seem fair that he would lose everything because of what Ronin had done. "I did everything you asked."

"You did," Agent Spear said. "But the mission isn't complete. You remember our deal? We need you. All your time with Ronin might yield something useful. You can help us bring him in."

Ben felt his rage returning, and took several deep breaths to keep from losing it.

"Something isn't adding up, here," Agent Taggart said. "It almost seems like this is what Ronin intended all along. As if he wanted to be caught, knowing we would send him undercover."

"But that would mean he knew about everything," Mr. Weathersky said. "Dr. Hughes. The Dread Cloaks. All of it."

"Or someone knew," Agent Spear said. "And they told Ronin."

The feeling of something itching at the edge of Ben's thoughts returned. The feeling he'd had before when he'd thought about that name. *Richter.* He thought back over the events of the last few weeks. The stranger helping Dr. Hughes. The anonymous tip about Ronin's jewel heist. The inside man Ronin didn't know well whom he had let on to his crew. The rival leader of the Dread Cloaks nobody knew. Could they all be related?

"Could it be Richter?" Ben asked.

Everyone in the room turned to look at him.

"I mean," Ben said, "could he be the someone behind it all?"

"We've been over this," Mr. Weathersky said. "Richter doesn't exist. Ronin does. Once again, let us focus on the devil we know. We need to capture him."

"That won't be easy," Agent Taggart said. "He knows exactly how to hide from us."

"We don't go after him," Mr. Weathersky said. He looked at Ben. "We draw him out. He'll bring the gun to us."

"Now, why would he do that?" Agent Spear asked.

"Because we have something he wants," Mr. Weathersky said. "Desperately."

Realization jolted through Ben. Ronin had been wrong. Mr. Weathersky hadn't lied, after all. "You really have her?"

"Have who?" Agent Taggart asked.

"His daughter," Mr. Weathersky said.

The two agents sat back in their chairs. They said nothing. Minutes passed.

"Are you sure about this?" Agent Spear said. "The risks —"

"Dr. Hughes," Mr. Weathersky said. "During your captivity among the Dread Cloaks, did you complete work on the augmenter gun? Ben told us you did not believe it to be reliable."

"No," she said. "But I did my best to look like I was trying to work on it. It is still very unpredictable, and I believe very dangerous."

Mr. Weathersky turned to Agent Spear. "You see? Whatever the risks, they are nothing compared to what a man like Morrow could do with that gun." Mr. Weathersky stood. "We have no choice." He turned to Ben. "And neither will Morrow."

"So where is his daughter?" Ben asked.

Mr. Weathersky leaned forward over the table, poised on his knuckles. "She's been training you and Peter. Sasha Lambert is Morrow's daughter."

CHAPTER
22

MR. Weathersky sent a personal message for Ronin out into the streets. Ben didn't hear what it was, exactly, but it had something to do with the night Ronin's wife had been murdered. Mr. Weathersky seemed convinced that it would work to lure the former agent in. After that, all they could do was wait for Ronin to make contact.

During that time, Ben and Peter didn't see much of Sasha. Their formal training had been suspended, but they practiced in the Big Top with the other agents, picking up tips and strategies from them where they could. Ben had rummaged through that same cardboard box and found another Locus to use, a tarnished silver dollar. He missed his old Locus, but this new one did the job.

Two days after Ronin had betrayed Ben, Ben sat with Peter in the dining room, spinning his Locus on the table. "I wish I could actuate without one."

"It's really not a big deal," Peter said. "Sasha was right; several agents use them."

"It's a big deal if you don't have one when you need it."

Peter took a bite of his sandwich, both elbows on the table. He seemed to have settled in too comfortably here. He had just accepted everything that had been done to them. He had bought in.

"They're just using you, you know," Ben said. "Me, too. They're controlling us."

"They're not controlling me," Peter said. "I want to be here."

Ben shook his head. "How could you —?"

But just then Sasha walked into the dining room, and Ben forgot what he was saying. He watched her as she crossed in front of the food warmers without taking anything, grabbed a bottle of water, and took a seat at a table by herself.

"Sasha." He got up and went over to her. "Are you okay?"

"Yeah," she said. "Fine."

"Haven't really seen you around much." Ben took a seat, and Sasha sat back, leaning away from him without making eye contact.

"No," she said. "I've been prepping for the operation."

"What kind of prep?" Peter had come over and took the seat next to Ben.

She rolled the water bottle between her hands. "Mostly how to handle Ronin."

"Is he really your father?" Peter asked.

Ben wanted to kick him under the table. Everything in Sasha's file made sense now. This was why she hadn't been detached. This was why there wasn't any info on her family or where she came from. But Ben remembered how she'd reacted when asked about this stuff before, and she didn't seem any more open to talking about it now.

"What do *you* think?" Sasha stared at Peter until he looked away.

"I — I don't know," he said. "I just —"

"Leave it alone," Ben said.

Sasha swung her stare onto him, and Ben offered her a gentle smile. She looked down at her water bottle, and then stood.

"I've got to go. See you two around."

She left the dining room, and after she was gone Peter shook his head.

"I don't get it."

"They're using her, too," Ben said. "Maybe she doesn't like it, either."

Mr. Weathersky's message reached its target, and apparently did a pretty good job of convincing him, because the next day, a package arrived at the League headquarters with instructions for the exchange.

"When and where?" Agent Spear asked.

"Tomorrow afternoon," Mr. Weathersky said. "Mercer Beach."

"Mercer Beach?" Ben could hear the panic in his own voice at the thought of going back there. "But that's where Poole is."

"Was," Agent Taggart said. "With the loss of the augmenter gun, he's left town. No one has seen him or heard from him since you freed Dr. Hughes."

"Right," Agent Spear said. "Poole was on his last leg, and you, son, knocked it out from under him." There was a hint of something in his voice. Pride?

"But . . ." Even with their reassurances, Ben didn't like this. "Couldn't this be some kind of trap?"

"He set no other terms," Mr. Weathersky said.

"Ronin is on his own," Agent Taggart said. "The Paracelsus crew will be after him, and so will the Dread Cloaks. He's getting desperate and careless. He might even *want* to be caught."

Ben doubted that very much.

"Perhaps," Mr. Weathersky said. "But we'll take no chances. I want a full contingency on this. Call in everyone you can."

"Yes, sir," Agent Taggart said.

"That includes you, Ben," Mr. Weathersky said. "And Peter. If you think you're ready."

The director's words blew across the embers of Ben's anger. Not just anger at Mr. Weathersky and the League, but anger at Ronin. "I'm ready," he said. "But I have one question."

"What's that?" Mr. Weathersky asked.

"What happens to Sasha?"

"Agent Lambert has been briefed. She's the bait, but we have no intention of actually letting Ronin take her."

Something about this didn't sit right. "But she's his daughter."

Mr. Weathersky paused. "Why don't you get to your point?"

"You're going to take her from him all over again."

"He did that to himself when he betrayed us."

Ben knew that. He knew Ronin was responsible, that he had no one to blame but himself. But Ronin was also a victim. The League had kept his daughter a secret, and rogue agent or not, that didn't seem right. But Ronin wasn't the only one they'd hurt. Sasha had gone through life without her father, maybe not even knowing who he was, and Ben couldn't imagine what that must have been like for her. That was the other kind of detachment she'd talked about that morning in the dining room.

"But you're also taking Sasha's dad away, too."

"We didn't force Agent Lambert to do this," Mr. Weathersky said. "She could have said no, but she chose to go ahead with the plan. So I suggest you worry less about other people and more about yourself. The retrieval of the augmenter gun is all you need concern yourself with."

But suddenly, Ben didn't like the idea of the augmenter gun in Mr. Weathersky's hands any more than he had in Poole's.

The next day, everyone suited up the way they had the night they went after the Paracelsus crew. Ben and Peter put on the same gear, and they loaded into similar vans, but this time, Sasha wasn't with them. Ben watched from inside his vehicle as she came out of the building with Mr. Weathersky, and they got into another car.

Ben reached forward and tapped Agent Spear's shoulder. "Is Mr. Weathersky coming?"

The agent nodded. "He sure is. Not often he gets into the action anymore."

Ben sat back and looked at Peter. Peter raised his eyebrow.

The cavalcade of a dozen vehicles pulled out and drove through the city along a route that had become familiar to Ben. Past downtown, out onto the highway, toward the refinery, then through the abandoned neighborhoods to Mercer Beach.

They drove under the old sign, and into the broken parking lot, where the vehicles spread out from a column to a wedge formation, barreling along beneath the twin shadows of the refinery towers, toward the park's entrance. Ben watched for any sign of an ambush. He searched for the red-and-black uniforms of the Dread Cloaks, but saw no sign of them.

The League vans came to a stop and the agents piled out. Between all the vehicles, there were fifty or sixty of them, and in their black assault gear they were a pretty intimidating force. Ben and Peter hung at the edge waiting for orders as Agents Spear and Taggart directed units of agents forward between the striped ticket booths into the park.

"Ben, Peter, you're with me." Mr. Weathersky walked toward them. Sasha marched beside him. "Stay close."

They followed the other agents down the main promenade, past the House of Mirrors and the carousel. A tense silence preceded and followed them, the only sounds those made by their feet and the rustle of their gear.

"Where are we going?" Ben whispered.

"Ronin wants to make the exchange in the arena," Mr. Weathersky said.

The arena seemed a very deliberate choice, and Ben's unease grew. He'd seen Ronin in action. Ben knew him well enough to know that the man would have a plan to avoid capture and get out of here, with his daughter and probably with the augmenter gun, too. But Ben did his best to suppress his fear and keep his breathing and his heart rate even.

When they arrived at the arena entrance, Ben reached into his pocket and clutched his Locus, the metal coin warm in his hand. Mr. Weathersky looked up at the building.

"I want everyone ready with actuations. Let's move." He led the way.

Agent Spear and Agent Taggart took up positions on either side of Ben, Peter, and Sasha as they moved forward through the arena doors. Ben felt the actuations stirring around him. He summoned up one of his own, a fireball, and his mind crackled with the potential of it.

Inside the arena, the air held still and the dim light strained to fill the space. In front of them, the open stage curtains spread darkness and shadows between them. Ben looked up at the control room, where Poole had made his office. The windows were black.

As the agents streamed into the building and fanned out, Mr. Weathersky strode to the middle of the performance ring. Agent Spear and Agent Taggart kept Ben, Peter, and Sasha back.

"Ronin!" Mr. Weathersky shouted. "It's over! Come out."

"Where is my daughter?" came Ronin's voice from somewhere up on the stage.

Ben squinted, but couldn't see anything. Ronin was definitely up to something. And if Ronin was desperate, who knew what that might be? Ben's unease climbed up a step into fear.

"She is among the agents, here." Mr. Weathersky gestured across the League forces. "But I will not reveal her to you until I have the augmenter gun in my hand."

"Is that so?" Ronin stepped forward on the stage into the light. He looked haggard, with dark rims under his eyes.

"And then what? You'll just hand over my daughter and let me go?"

"Come now, Ethan," Mr. Weathersky said. "You know how this will play out. You knew it when you came here. But you came anyway."

"You're right," Ronin said.

He had a confident glint in his eyes. Ben had seen that look before, back at the abandoned house. Ronin had laid a trap somehow. Ben looked over his shoulder at the exit. He touched Sasha's arm, and she turned to look at him.

"Something is wrong," he whispered.

He couldn't read her expression, but he was aware that her father stood up there, the father she had never known. What was she feeling? Ben didn't like the idea of giving Ronin what he wanted, but Sasha had a right to know her father.

He turned to Peter. "Be ready to run."

Peter nodded.

"Where is the portable augmenter, Ethan?" Mr. Weathersky asked.

Ronin looked up into the rafters and catwalks overhead. "Well, I didn't think it was fair to just hand it over to you. There are a number of interested parties. So I thought I'd give you all a sporting chance."

Mr. Weathersky took a step forward. "What do you —?"

But he stopped, and Ben felt why. Actuations blazed to life above them, and combined with the actuations held at the ready by the League agents, the arena felt charged enough to explode. There was an army up there at least as big as the force of League agents. This was an ambush. But who were they?

"Is that Poole?" Mr. Weathersky asked.

"Poole is gone," Ronin said. "But the Dread Cloaks remain with a new leader."

"The rival that drove Poole out?" Mr. Weathersky said.

Ronin shrugged. "Does it matter?"

"What happens now?" Mr. Weathersky asked.

Ronin pulled the augmenter gun out from behind his back. "I'm going to put this here." He bent over and set the gun on the stage. "And I'm going to let you all fight it out."

Ben's darting gaze turned frantic. This was going to be a massive firefight. He had to get Sasha out of there. Peter, too. He grabbed them both by the arm and pulled them toward the door. Peter caught on and came on his own, but he had to tug on Sasha.

The League agents had turned their attention upward, but in the shadows they didn't know what or who to aim at. The Dread Cloaks had the advantage. Ronin backed away from the augmenter gun with his hands raised.

"You have a choice, Old One," he said, approaching the shadows. "You can follow me, or you can try to keep the augmenter out of Dread Cloak hands." As he disappeared behind the stage, he made eye contact with Ben. Then he looked at Sasha. He smiled again, and faded away.

"Agents," Mr. Weathersky said, "be —"

The air filled with a deafening explosion as lightning, fire, and ice shot down, striking the arena floor and a few League agents. They all scrambled for cover, returning fire randomly. Mr. Weathersky charged fearlessly through the barrage toward the stage.

"Let's get out of here!" Ben shouted. He led the way, Peter and Sasha behind him.

They raced out into the amusement park, and Ben looked around for a place they could hide. Once Mr. Weathersky got his hands on the augmenter, he would try to get it out of there, and the battle would move outside. He needed to find a safe place for them before that happened.

"But the League," Sasha said. "My friends."

"Let them fight it out over that augmenter," Ben said. "That was Mr. Weathersky's choice. You don't owe them anything, especially after what they did to you."

Sasha looked back through the doors, clearly torn.

"Look," Ben said. "I think Ronin will come find us. You are what's most important to him."

"I think Ben is right," Peter said.

Ben looked around for a place they could go to hide and wait. One of the other buildings, maybe. The House of Mirrors was the closest.

"This way," he said.

Sasha shook her head. "But —"

Ben looked at Peter, and together they pulled Sasha along between them. When they reached the building, they found the doors locked, but Ben kicked them open. The doors burst inward, and the three of them went inside.

They were in an open, mirrored entryway, with two hallways leading off to either side. "We'll wait here," Ben said. "Ronin will find us."

"No." Sasha pulled off her helmet and dug her fingers through her hair. "No, you don't understand."

"Don't understand what?" Peter asked.

"Ronin is not my father."

CHAPTER
23

"**WHAT?**" Ben said.

Sasha started pacing around the House of Mirrors entryway. "Ronin is not my father."

Peter cocked his head. "But —"

"It was Mr. Weathersky's idea," she said. "The League never had Ronin's daughter. But we had to find a way to get the portable augmenter back."

Ben's stomach fell. Mr. Weathersky had lied again, and he had lied about the very thing Ben had thought he wouldn't. Even Ronin had believed him. It didn't seem like there was anything the League wouldn't do.

This wasn't right. For Ronin, this would be like killing his daughter all over again.

Ben looked hard at Sasha. "You went along with this?"

"They were my orders," she said. "I didn't have a choice."

"And what about other kinds of detachment? You lied to me?"

"No. That is still true."

"But —"

"Now is not the time, Ben."

She was right. They had to deal with Ronin first. "We can't do this to him. We have to hide you."

"Hide where?" Sasha asked.

Ben looked down the nearest hallway. "Deeper inside the building. Come on."

The three of them dove ahead, into a mirrored corridor. But the angles had already started to fragment what they were seeing, splitting and multiplying, casting the reflections of endless edges and passages away from them. They slowed down, but pressed forward, entering a chamber where Ben almost wanted to grab onto Sasha and Peter to remind himself which were the real ones and which were the illusions.

They went down another passageway, and entered a second chamber, and then a third. That was when they heard a distant voice.

"Ben?"

It was Ronin.

"I know you're in here," he said. "I saw the door kicked in. You have my daughter?"

Ben put his fingers to his lips, and Sasha and Peter nodded. They held still, listening.

"Just give me my daughter," Ronin said. "Please. You, of all people, know what this means. What the League did to me."

His voice moved. It sounded as though he had entered the hallway.

"I'm sorry for taking off the way I did," Ronin said. "I had to make sure Mr. Weathersky would make good on his promise. The augmenter was the only leverage I had."

He was coming toward them, getting closer.

"I'm not going to hurt you," he said. "Please."

Ben wondered if they should get actuations ready. Ronin would sense that, and it might give them away. But he was going to find them at any moment. The building only had the illusion of size, and there were really only a few feet and a few mirrors between them and him.

Ben was trying to decide which actuation to summon, when Ronin's voice came from just around the corner.

"I only want to see her," he said.

Then Ronin came around the corner, and he stopped short. He stared at Sasha. Tears welled up in his eyes.

"Stay back!" Peter shouted.

But Ronin acted as if he hadn't even heard him, and came into the chamber.

Ben sensed Peter readying an actuation, and he reached out and grabbed him. "Don't."

Peter looked back and forth between Ben and Ronin, and Ben felt the energy dissipate.

Ronin walked up to Sasha and looked down at her. She held her ground, looking back up at him. He smiled, and seemed to be studying her face, looking at both sides. He looked directly into her eyes for a long while. But gradually, the smile he wore faded away. The tears in his eyes dried up. His head and shoulders fell.

"You're not," he whispered.

Sasha shook her head. "How could you tell?"

"I see none of my wife in you. None of my daughter's mother."

"I'm sorry," Sasha whispered.

Ronin said nothing, and several minutes passed.

Ben wanted to say something to him, but there was nothing that would comfort him. Nothing that could bring his daughter back. Just like there was nothing Ben could say to his mother to remind her who he was.

From outside the building, they heard a sudden boom. Sasha and Peter flinched. The battle must have spilled out of the arena. Ronin straightened and looked at Ben.

"I'm sorry, kid," he said. "I'm sorry for what the League did to you."

"What about what you did to me?" Ben stepped toward him. "The League refused to reattach me to my mom until they get the augmenter gun back. And you stole it!"

"Kid." Ronin put both hands on Ben's shoulders. "I want you to listen carefully to me. The League lied to you. They can't reattach you. Detachment is not reversible."

Ben's vision started to go dark at the edges, turning into a tunnel. At the center, Ronin's rough face looked at him with an expression of pity, but everything else was a blur. He started feeling light-headed. This could not be happening. All he'd worked for, all he'd done. Detachment couldn't be permanent.

"You're lying," Ben whispered.

"I'm not," Ronin said. "I've got no reason to lie to you. But the League had every reason to tell you what you wanted to hear."

Shock caught the words in Ben's throat, and stuck his mouth shut. He just stared.

"Ben," Peter said. "I'm so sorry."

"Me, too," Sasha said.

There wasn't anything to be sorry for. This couldn't be true. Maybe Ronin didn't think detachment was reversible, but that didn't mean it was true. The League could reattach him. They *had* to.

"I'm sorry, too," Ronin said. "All of this for something that doesn't even work."

"What?" Peter asked.

"The portable augmenter doesn't work," Ronin said. "I spent days trying, and it never did anything. It's not just unreliable. It's not functional."

"But . . ." Ben recovered his voice. He rubbed his head. "I used it. It worked for me."

"Not as an augmenter," Ronin said. "Maybe it worked like a Locus for you. You just didn't realize it." He turned away from them. "I'm getting out of here, somewhere the League will never find me. But before I go, let me just say this, kid. Now that you know the truth about everything, what you do from here is up to you. You're not their hostage anymore."

Ronin left.

The word echoed in Ben's mind. *Hostage.* That was the truth of it. The League had kept Ben in a kind of prison, using what was most important to him to control him. Well, he was done being controlled. He was breaking free. Right now.

He turned to look at Peter and Sasha. "You might not want to come with me."

"Where are you going?" Peter asked.

"To find out the truth." Ben stalked away from them, back through the mirrored hallways to the entryway, and then out into the park, right into the middle of a battle.

Quantum League agents and Dread Cloaks had taken up defensive positions around the promenade, behind booths and buildings, exchanging fire. Actuations flew between them. Walls shattered and exploded. Agents and Dread Cloaks fell. The air smelled of ozone from all the lightning and smoke from all the fireballs. The carousel was in a blaze nearby, the horses seeming to writhe in a fiery death.

Ben pulled out his Locus. He stared at it in his hand. Then he tossed it to the ground. He didn't need it. It didn't control him, either. He was not at the mercy of anyone, or anything. From now on, he controlled himself.

He closed his eyes and reached for the storm churning inside him. All the pain and all the anger. He wound it all together, pulling the vortex tighter and tighter. He imagined the air around him getting hot, the molecules jostling and bouncing off one another, generating friction. This heat rose up, through the cooler air above it, and he stretched the column tight, setting it rotating. Faster, and faster, fueled by the energy of his own spinning world.

He opened his eyes.

A whirlwind towered before him, as tall as the Ferris wheel. Its foot clawed at the ground, raking up dirt and debris and sending it shooting upward and outward. Ben held the tornado in place for a moment longer, noticing that the battle had stopped. He would show them all.

He released the whirlwind, and it charged forward, striking the first building. The shriek of splintering wood filled the air as it tore the booth to pieces. Then it moved on to the next building, voracious, and destroyed it, too.

Agents and Dread Cloaks scattered before it.

Who was in control now?

"Ben!" Peter had followed him outside, and stood beside him. "You have to stop this!"

"Why?" Ben asked. "After what they did to you and me? Why should I stop this?"

"Some of them are my friends!" Sasha said on his other side. She grabbed him. "Stop this before you hurt someone!"

"Hurt someone? They were killing each other out here! The Dread Cloaks would have killed me!" Ben shouted. "The League detached me!"

The tornado kept going, annihilating everything in its path.

"But this isn't the way!" Sasha said. "You're hurting good people, too!"

She was right. Some of the agents might even be like him: angry, betrayed, and confused. He hadn't stopped to think about them until now. Hadn't stopped to think about the cost. That was something Mr. Weathersky would do. Not Ben. When he realized that, the storm inside him broke apart. The anger faded, even though the pain remained.

But the tornado kept going.

Ben closed his eyes and reached out for it with his consciousness. He felt for the air currents, and imagined the temperature above the cyclone rising, throwing off the difference in pressure that kept the whirlwind going. He imagined it scattering in the same way he'd imagined it forming.

But when he opened his eyes, it was still there.

He closed his eyes and tried again. He failed.

He couldn't undo the actuation. It raged on, tearing and breaking and shattering everything it seized, and he remembered the warning Dr. Hughes had given him that day in her office. That this power could get away from him. That he could lose control of it.

He turned to Peter. "I can't stop it."

"Look!" Sasha pointed.

Some distance away from them, Mr. Weathersky strode forward down the middle of the promenade toward the tornado. Then he stopped, buffeted by the winds, closed his eyes, and lifted his hands into the air. Ben could feel the force and strength of the actuation Mr. Weathersky summoned from where he stood.

Moments later, the tornado went to tatters, dropping its debris to the ground, and it vanished.

The silent aftermath didn't last long before the Dread Cloaks began a retreat, scattering in all directions. Some of the League agents regrouped and pursued them. Others began actuating rain and water to extinguish the fires burning around them. But Mr. Weathersky stood where he was. He turned toward Ben.

Ben took a deep breath. It was time for the truth. He left the House of Mirrors and marched toward the Old One.

"That was a Class Three actuation, Ben," Mr. Weathersky said as Ben approached him. "I had no idea of your potential."

Ben ignored him. "You have the portable augmenter. Now reattach me."

Mr. Weathersky put his hands in his pockets. "Ben —"

"REATTACH ME!"

"I can't," Mr. Weathersky said. "Reattachment isn't possible. I'm sorry."

Ben thought about Agent Spear's promise. He thought about Mr. Weathersky, and the lies he had told Ronin, realizing that he had been blind to the lies the Old One had told him because he hadn't wanted to know the truth.

The truth was that his mom didn't know him anymore. He had never even existed to her.

The truth was that she was alone.

Ben was alone.

Tears rose, and an emptiness spread through him. He became a shell, as fragile as an empty egg, ready to shatter at the slightest touch.

"I'm sorry, Ben," Mr. Weathersky said. "We did what we needed to do for the good of everyone. We will continue to do so. That is the mandate of the Quantum League."

"It isn't my mandate," Ben said. "And I won't be a part of it."

"What are you saying?" Mr. Weathersky asked.

"I'm leaving," Ben said.

"You can't," Mr. Weathersky said. "Someone with your potential must be —"

"Are you going to stop me?" Ben felt the emptiness inside him filling back up, but with the same pain and anger that had produced the tornado. "You want another Class Three on your hands? An even bigger one?"

Mr. Weathersky swallowed.

Ben walked away from him, preparing for the director to try to attack him. But he felt no actuations rising. Nothing. Ben kept going, but a few steps later, Peter and Sasha stepped in front of him.

"Don't go," Peter said.

"I have to," Ben said. "This is my choice. Now that Dr. Hughes is safe, there's nothing left for me here." He paused. He knew how that sounded. Peter was his friend. "Why don't you come with me?"

Peter's eyes watered. "I — I can't. This is where I belong."

Ben nodded. "Okay, then."

"Please," Sasha said. "Stay."

"I'm sorry." Ben pushed between them both. Sasha had been right. There were other kinds of detachment, and they were just as real. They hurt just as bad.

"Where will you go?" she asked.

"I don't know." He looked back at them, and beyond them to Mr. Weathersky. "I'm going to find a way to reattach myself."

There had to be a way, and Ben would discover it. He turned his back on his friends, and marched forward through the smoldering, broken remains of the Mercer Beach amusement park. No one tried to stop him, but he knew this wasn't the last he would see of the League. Maybe he would even have to go into hiding like Ronin.

He came to the park gates, and passed through them, into the parking lot. It would be a long walk back to the city, but Ben knew where he belonged. He just had to find a way to get there.

ACKNOWLEDGMENTS

There are many people I would like to thank for their continued love and support: Lisa Sandell, my editor and dear friend, for going with me as I tried something new and different once again, and for helping shape the book into what it is; Stephen Fraser, my agent, for the vision he had for my career from the beginning; my family, for accepting me as I am, unconditionally; my friends, who I am reluctant to name for fear of forgetting someone, but who each enrich my life in distinct and beautiful ways.

I cannot imagine being detached from any of you.

ABOUT THE AUTHOR

Matthew J. Kirby is the critically acclaimed author of the middle-grade novels *Icefall*, which won the Edgar Award for Best Juvenile Mystery and the PEN Literary Award for Children's and Young Adult Literature; *The Clockwork Three*, which was named a *Publishers Weekly* flying start; *The Lost Kingdom*; and *Cave of Wonders*, the fifth book in the Infinity Ring series. He was born in Utah and grew up in Maryland, California, and Hawaii. Matthew lives in Utah, where he is working on his next novel.

Visit his website at www.matthewjkirby.com.